I0557942

The One About
the Boy and Nothing

Ankur Bhanderi

Copyright © 2023 Ankur Bhanderi.

All rights reserved.

This is a work of fiction. Names, characters, places, and incidents are products of the author's imagination or are used fictitiously and are not to be construed as real. Any resemblance to actual events, locales, organizations, or persons, living or dead, is entirely coincidental.

No part of this book may be reproduced, or stored in a retrieval system, or transmitted in any form or by any means, electronic, mechanical, photocopying, recording, or otherwise, without express written permission of the publisher.

ISBN 979-8-9879584-2-1

Cover design by: Ankur Bhanderi
Printed in the United States of America

M, S

Have you heard the one about the boy and nothing?

Well… You wouldn't get it.

Besides, as jokes go, there's nothing there.

Heh. That's all I have.

I slept until the poisonous sun went down, skipped my shift, and dreamed I went to sea and never was found. It's chilly out here, and damp, and November in San Diego. The sky is a beautiful gradient of deep horizon yellows to blues, to drowned, back to sleep.

I love this time of day, the dusky nowhen between two worlds. It's fully empty. Empty, despite yourself. Empty, despite evening traffic white noising just a few blocks away. Empty, despite an unseen beast approaching on the sidewalk up ahead.

By the time I can make out the dim shape of a man, I'm already slipping into the parking lot for what appears to be a biotech company. This stupid myopia doesn't hold me back anymore. Sometimes I can act on the psychic pressure, that disturbance in the air when someone's invading my personal plot. You know what I'm talking about, right? Right? Bullshit, I'm sure, but, seen or not, I slip invaders' eyes with such intuition that I can't help but fantasize.

Dimly, I can make out a pale button-down shirt and ill-fitting, beige dork-slacks. I'm camouflaged against the city's twilight in dark grays and blues, colors to disappear in without the appearance of intent. Who wears the night better, do you think?

I pull out a cigarette, and let a kind of uninteresting and uninterested world-weariness descend on my shoulders. Hunched against the coming night at the requisite distance from an unwindowed side door, I'm just some tired second-shift man who puffs, puffs, puffs on his smoke break, and I may as well be invisible.

The office drone walks by. He's playing music on his phone, out loud, without headphones, for all the night to hear. Rude. He looks at me, but more in my direction than at me. I register in his mind for only a moment; I can almost feel his attention slipping away until, to him, I'm gone and have always been gone and have always never been to begin with.

And then he's gone. And then I stop being the softly beaten down technician and resume being me. Or, at least, someone I think is me. Can you even be sure?

Have you heard the one about the kid who memorized at least four jokes to introduce himself but couldn't for the life or death of him remember to tell even one?

Well. Like most people my age, I'm twenty-one. Jace: Jason Choi, for short: too short, too skinny, too bent, great hair, disheveled, eyes not too chinky although dead like a soldier's. But you've heard this one before, right? You *are* listening?

I suppose I'll have to say something worth hearing first.

Someday.

I continue up the now empty street and turn onto Miramar. As I walk down the road, it smells alternately of a refreshing mountain spring and a potent fart. It's a frustrating olfactory journey of tension and release, tension and release... if that sort of thing floats, rocks, harbors, or sinks your boat... if you have a boat to begin with.

A right turn beyond the third mountain spring and a long, shallow descent past various nearly identical corporate campuses brings me to a recessed area tucked into the back end of an office building, which one might expect to house a loading dock or dumpster but instead has a café.

Have you heard of such a thing?

Granted, I don't know shit about what factors into the differentiation between a successful eatery and an array of boarded up windows, but they say that thing about three locations, and this must be at least the fourth or fifth…

I appreciate it, of course. I appreciate the secrecy, the sheer underworldliness of it. But who else would? Well, I assume *someone* would. The restaurant must, in fact, still be open for business during the daybright, 9-5er hours when I'm liable to be found sleeping, if at all. But it's deserted right now.

They have this lovely patio with tables and benches arranged beneath strings of white lights that look like tiny stars. When they're on, at least. Some disappointer must have pulled the plug tonight. The small change in lighting turns the whole place into a half-remembered dreamscape. Everything is vague and vaguely peculiar. I walk to my bench anyway.

The patio overlooks a sprawling parking lot lined with manicured trees, with slender, towering lamps that reach me here in beams of stark blue-white light and long, impenetrable shadows. My footsteps echo over the empty grid of white paint, are slow to fade, eventually give way to a heavy silence that seems to echo itself.

There's a kind of holy desolation to the place, to most all abandoned places. It's beautiful and sad and becoming a part of it makes it easier to forget how terrifying it is from the outside.

I sit. I watch. The night holds me in its cold arms.

"What are you doing here?"

I freeze.

The voice is light, almost bright, a little jarring as it echoes around my hollow corner of night. I can't tell where it's coming from. Without moving, I scan the patio before me for the source and see no one.

The voice is a woman's, but I see no woman, or falsetto-man, or anyone at all. It must be a security guard from the building behind me.

This has never happened to me here before. They're not supposed to actually *catch* me. Maybe they've been watching me all this time and finally killed the lights to discourage me? But they would've seen then that I'm not doing any—

"Why are you here?" the voice asks again, from all angles.

"I-I'm going," I say, getting up slowly to give myself time to find the guard. My voice bounces back to me in a confusing reverb and I almost lose track of where *I* am. I show my empty hands and assure the phantom guard, in as unthreatening a tone as I can manage, "I'll go. No problem. No harm done."

I stand and turn in a smooth, apparently careless motion, and I still don't see anyone. I wish I'd brought my glasses. I wish it weren't so damn dark. I wish I were anywhere else. I wish...

I shift my weight, stretch, casually cast my desperate gaze into every shadow.

"You don't have to *leave*... Just wondering why you're here."

What a shit security guard.

I turn in a slow circle, abandoning any effort to look as if I'm not looking.

"You look lost," I hear, from a hundred ghost voices whirling and mocking and jeering all around me. But there's no one God damn here!

"Who are you?" I ask.

"Sometimes I think this is a lost people kind of place," all the ghosts answer.

That's not an answer. That's not an answer at all. I don't know what that means and I'm not sure how I'm supposed to respond to it. So, I say:

"Have you heard the one about the couple lost in the night?"

"What?"

"This couple, a man and a woman, go for a hike and end up lost in the woods after dark. They're making their way back to the road but their progress is slow since the night is pitch black and all they have is a dinky flashlight to shine.

"As they make their way along in the darkness, the woman starts to get nervous. All the wild noises around them sound to her like voices, like approaching feet, like danger and death and every lurking corner. She whispers to her boyfriend, 'I think someone's out there. Following us.'

"'You're just imagining things,' he says. 'There's no one here but us. I'll prove it.' Louder, to the darkness, he shouts, 'Is anyone out there?'

"'God, I hope not,' the darkness replies. 'I'm fucking spooked.'"

The night is silent for a long moment. I stay where I am, searching, waiting. Have I ever even been in the woods? I mean, really in the woods, where there are no signs of human life anywhere to be seen. It sounds like a dream, you know?

Finally, the voice returns, bouncing all around and back to me:

"What the fuck was that?"

I see a sudden movement, to my left. A shape, now separated from the surrounding darkness by the motion of arms thrown up in the air. It rises, moves, makes itself so obvious that I'm a little ashamed to be alive and so blind. Not fifteen feet away, on the far side of a table skewered through by a large umbrella, there's standing the silhouette of a woman.

"I—ahh. It was…" I stammer. It was just a joke.

"Were you talking to the dark?" the shape asks, walking toward me around the tables. "Did you think I was a fucking spooky night demon?"

She steps across the sharp blue-white line between light and dark and I see a long young woman, with a long, blue-white face and long, blue-white hair. Below her baggy hoodie, her shorts reveal long, blue-white legs. She's thin, but looks as if that were an accident. She's taller than me, and looks as if that were on purpose, out of spite. The bitch.

"You totally did," she says. "You walked right past me and sat down like you were all by yourself, told your stupid story, spun around like a blind dog chasing its tail. Anything you can't see is just a fucking moon wizard talking to you, right?"

Fine. Maybe I did. But this seems unnecessary.

"No," I say. "I was just joking."

"Oh my god," she laughs. She won't even do me the courtesy of looking doubtful, skipping straight to cruel mockery. Rude.

"I just like jokes..."

She laughs right past my comment, bent double, and goes on for what feels to me like an unreasonably long time. I don't know what I'm supposed to do while she finishes this whole bit she's doing.

I study her face as she cackles. Her mouth is too wide. Her lips are too thin. Her eyes are too big, although adequately dark. She might have freckles but it's hard to tell in this light.

Finally, she stops laughing, and wipes at her eyes, and stares at me, skeptically, perhaps, or critically, or with the impassive curiosity of a scientist. Is there crap on my face? Is my mouth the wrong size? Or my eyes? It's the eyes, isn't it?

She says, matter-of-factly, "You don't know how to talk to people."

"Because I don't insult people I don't even know?"

"Yes. Exactly. You should find someone to teach you, before it's too late."

What does that even mean? We watch each other for a time.

"Emma," she says.

"Jace." I hold out my hand. She doesn't take it.

"Jace?"

"Yeah."

"What kind of name is *Jace*?"

"Nickname," I explain. Why can't anyone ever just accept it? "For Jason."

She doesn't respond beyond a thoughtful grunt. I ask, "What are you doing here?"

"Ladies first."

"What?"

"I asked first, stupid."

"I—I don't know. I just—I come here sometimes. I've never seen *you* here before."

"You barely saw me here tonight." She smirks to herself a little; one of her eyebrows goes up for a second. "I go places. Big deal."

"But why *here*?"

"What?"

"Why here?"

"It's nice here. Why shouldn't I? You don't own it. Why do *you* come here?"

Fine.

"I own it."

She looks me up and down. "Yeah, I bet."

"Fine. It's nice," I admit.

I don't know how to ask her to stay, to sit and to talk and to just be present, but not in the pathetically needy way that you know I mean it. I start to speak but she interrupts me.

"Listen, Jason. I've got to run. I'll see you around, maybe, yeah?"

"Jace. Will you?"

"Sure," she says. I don't believe her.

"Jason," she says. I don't like her.

Emma throws a hand up to her brow in ironic salute as she turns to leave. She strides across the near corner of the blue-white parking lot on long, blue-white legs. I think about creeping after her, but she power-walks through a gap between two trees and is gone before my slow brain can decide what to do.

I wonder what kind of house we'd live in if we were to get married.

That's weird. Don't do that.

I hope I see her again.

I know I'm being weird, but I would have decided to not stalk her, given the time to actually decide.

For the record.

If you're keeping notes.

The pale grass billows in a strong prairie wind, from horizon to horizon, undulating and enchanting and haunting as reality denied. Above us, a uniform battlefield gray, marching along with the currents and never breaking formation for a second. It should rain again. I should hope.

Dad drives with both hands on the wheel, a huge grin painted on his face, with frequent glances back to catch us awed, to catch us laughing together, to catch us up in his passage.

Mama's not here. I'm not sure if he's noticed that she's gone.

The hills roll all around us. We roll between them, up and over, threatening on the far side to slip under but pulling up just in the very, very nick of time. The grasses part before our enormous truck, breaking and crashing upon the prow.

"Could a *road* ever take you here?" Dad asks again. I don't know, I want to tell him, but can't or can't bring myself to. But the road must be long, long gone by now in the rearview. Dad tells us not to look back. As if I wanted to see the ruin in our wake anyway. Anyway, where's Mama?

Dad tells us that the bad years are behind us now, literally, of course, I'm to understand, but now truly and finally and forget about it, kiddo, okay? because we're out of it and we've weathered the storm and we're out of it and we're never looking back, no sir, no *sir.*

The verdure whispers its agreement as it passes beneath and around the hull. Hisses and rustles and the faintest of crunches that make me wince. Sporadic, hollow rattles below. The small crack of a pebble bouncing off the roof. The light dims.

Another small crack, and another. The clouds, heavy now, brooding now, bellow and crash as suddenly the storm breaks and we're submersed in the womb of the cloudburst. Mother titans drop drowsy handfuls of gravel upon tin ceilings.

Mama?

All other sounds are drowned out and it makes me feel sleepy and giddy and relief like I've never known. We laugh. Even Dad. My god, we laugh so hard. The windblown howling of the gale sucks up our laughter greedily and demands more, more. And we laugh, my god.

Another hill crested and for a moment I see a landscape transformed. The grass has deepened profoundly, grown darker, longer, greener, stronger, unfathomable, fathomless, orphic in its savageness. Naturally, we exult over this new life. It's truly the most beautiful thing I've ever seen. Then it's gone. All I see is the streaming water and the greenest grass flowing all around us, higher now than my little porthole can see.

Sometimes blue-white flashes pierce the jade tapestry outside but the sound is constant. We bounce over a rough patch and are thrown to one side of the cabin. Dad turns to check on us, finds us hysterical. He's no longer steering at all and our laughter becomes indistinguishable from the thunderous roar around us.

We peak again and the downpour has become a thick curtain. It allows only fleeting glimpses of the flourishing world behind it.

A fulminous host. Unending thunder. Tears of laughter streak our faces as we go under. The plunge over the hill is so smooth that it feels like the vessel's floating, floating on air. We're swallowed by grasses that stretch over and wrap us up in a cocoon that transmutes tempest to distant cachinnation, a hazy, delirious echo of our own.

We laugh so hard, my god. Dad tumbles half into the back seat with us as he cracks all up and down and diagonalways and we all hang onto each other to keep from falling overboard.

All around us are stalks of the deepest, deepest green, the closest and most comforting night, hints of hints of precious refracted light in shades of emerald and sapphire.

I call for Mama; she would hate to miss this.

I'm calling for Mama but only howls escape my lips.

We laugh so hard, my god, I can't even breathe.

Irregular rays of sunset stab at my eyes through the shitty broken blinds. They rattle together faintly with a light evening wind. I'm not exactly proud of sleeping through the entirety of yet another day, but it's worse still to rise just in time to witness the shadows execute the last ray.

Have you heard the one about the sun and the sleeping god?

At the end of the longest night that live comedy had never seen, Leto called, "Rise and shine, son!" And so he did.

Stupid.

My phone stops making noise. It's the kind that you have to flip open. I got that one on purpose.

I dreamed we were sailing an ocean of grass laughing and the last eleven years had never happened.

It starts up with the noises again. I answer. Jorge reminds me in his broken English of my shift tonight because, out of a kind of cowardly politeness, I pretend that I forget and not, not care.

Fine. I'll go. My voice comes out a feeble croak. I haven't spoken in two days. Emma hasn't been back to my underworld café in two nights.

It's not like I've been holding my breath.

I laze for a bit longer after hanging up before dragging myself out of bed. My toes hurt. My sigh is a curling wisp of algid mist and it finally smells like winter.

I hop onto my beige computer—beige makes the oldest computers. I delete another seven emails about that trip to Bermuda that I won in a contest I never entered, each one more insistent than the last that this is absolutely real, no fibbing, they swear. I check in on the various internet loser forums I regularly lurk, the ones populated by deranged schizoids with no girlfriends. I'm not like them at all, you understand, but they make me laugh.

And that's a good half-hour wasted, not entirely on purpose. I haven't much time at this point to wash, dress, walk, wait, smoke, shiver, board, but now I'm en route and the burden of punctuality is blissfully out of my hands.

A man on the bus sneers at me in a mild way. Rude. I surreptitiously check my clothes, fix my hair, examine the size of my eyes in reflection, decide that I don't know why. Why, though?

I straighten my back and look disinterestedly out the window, trying to be someone who doesn't get sneered at and wouldn't mind either way. But I also take careful note of how he looks—bloated, brown, sneering, too much hair in and below the ears and too little above, square glasses, pretentious peacoat, *sneering*—so that I can later forget him all the more completely. That'll show him.

I affix myself to a chromed pole on the bus because I know I ought to give up my seat for the pregnant, old, crippled, fat, lazy, smelly, feline, but I fancy I know myself and I know I'd likely find myself paralyzed with discomfort at the thought of actually taking action, should one of those happen to board. A few of them do. They take vacant seats without hesitation. Crisis averted.

A teenager sitting near me takes, by my count, eight identical photos of himself. For what? I hope he keeps them all. Eight is a good number.

Have you heard the one about seven, eight, nine?

Good one.

It takes a little under forty-five minutes and a little over one bus transfer to get to work. The mousy lady with the lazy eye who womans the front desk doesn't look up when I sign in. I don't know her name but—and keep this between us—I call her Anne Frank in my head, because she looks like the type of person who would hide from Nazis in an attic.

I walk through the cafeteria full of men waiting for something good to finally happen in their lives and make my way back into the kitchen.

Jorge nods. I nod. We collect. We wash. We dry. I spray. Jorge clears out the steamer thing, standing on his tippy-toes to reach the ones in the back. The bums sometimes thank me as they hand me their trays. I don't particularly want to hear it but I won't deny them the hideous pleasure of gratitude in their bleak, tray-dinner lives.

One man, the only Asian in line, asks what I am, with that unique warmth reserved for aliens encountering strangers of the same shade. He has the stolid, lined face of a hard-working Christian patriarch, who retired to a quaint sidewalk on National Avenue after a lifetime of abusing his children. And he walks away sighing with indignation before I can finish telling him that I'm only fractionally Korean.

Rude. I can see why his kids don't take him in.

Today's volunteers are young, sexy, and hip. They appear to be white collar officemates, and not one acknowledges Jorge or me as they walk in.

Why did the man sneer at me?

They laugh, flirt, live, and feel good about themselves as they plop small squares of cornbread and beef patty stew onto trays. I hate them a little bit—I know I shouldn't—but fuck them—for the way they laugh, flirt, sneer, live, plop, ignore, feel good.

I listen without looking up. If I'm to be excluded, I deny them the hideous pleasure of excluding me.

Does Jorge feel the same way about them? He never really seems to feel any sort of way, not when I'm around. I'm afraid to ask, in case it makes him feel some sort of way about me.

The sexy volunteers finish up and leave, patting every which back—not ours, naturally—with the satisfaction of knowing that they'll never have to come back to this purgatoryhole.

Meanwhile, Jorge and I hit our night's peak. We work at a feverish, mindless pace. We collect. We wash. We dry. Another bum thanks us with a sort of pleading look in his eyes. I don't know what he wants but I don't think I have it.

Have you heard the one about the beggar at the light?

There was a beggar. He stood at the base of a traffic light. He had a cardboard sign, and it said something awfully pitiful. When the light turned red, a man in a high-end car came to a stop and rolled down his window.

"I think, my friend, I could spare $20 to help you out," the man said, rifling through his wallet.

"Thank you! You're so very generous, sir," the beggar replied ecstatically. "God bless!"

"Then again," the man said, rifling further, "What's to say you won't just spend this on dope? I know how you people are... Maybe I'll give you $10. That ought to be enough for a meal, right?"

"Oh... Yeah. Sure. Yeah. Thank you, sir. God bless, sir!"

Rifling further still, the man then said, "Well, if I give you $10, won't that incentivize you to keep begging instead of finding real, honest work? Maybe $5 is the way to go."

At this point, the beggar had lost hope and started walking away to try the next car in line, but the man called out to him.

"Hey! Where are you going? You owe me $5!"

But why did the man sneer?

After we finish, we make our to-go trays with wrinkled fingers and damp sleeves. Jorge's wife picks him up in a beat-up old car. It's green. I think green makes reliable cars.

Jorge nods. I nod. We don't speak much and that suits me fine, but I do enjoy the way he pronounces my name on the rare occasions he does. "Hyace."

Jorge came up through the program and he's doing well for himself now. He's married and I think her name is Benita and he works several jobs and that's probably always been his American Dream. We don't speak much and that really does suit me fine, but he knows I exist and minds when I don't show up because it's a lot of work for a single person, even though he's married.

I don't know how he managed before the day I showed up. I'm still not sure what I thought I would find here, but I panicked when they started explaining the program too fast and I told them that I was just looking for work. They must have seen in me something that would make a man on the bus sneer, and an Emma not come back for three days, and a you not pay attention, so they gave me a job washing dishes for dinner. Between that and housemates I avoid and not doing things and some light thievery—you know he deserved it—I just barely have a home.

So, I've that going for me, at least.

Outside, I watch through clouds of breath the green car disappearing around a corner. I watch a box truck with swordfish tattoos coming back the other way. I watch the road with bated breath as it waits and waits and waits for the weight of any other vehicle, but... It's an empty start to an empty evening. My seething heart tempts me to empty it, depart, and leave it freezing.

Then again, my food might get cold.

I eat and smoke by myself in a corner of the small, barely paved parking lot. It should be at least eleven minutes before the next bus arrives, I expect. The shelter doors have shut for the night and the stragglers have cleared out, off to sleep on a street appropriately distant from the organization determined to keep them from sleeping on a street—there's something funny about that. Don't you think so?

There are some cars near the entrance to the building. Odd. How many cars might one expect to find at a homeless shelter? Three, if one knows what to expect, I expect. Four, in seven minutes, if that counts. But I expect it doesn't count.

Have you heard the one about my dead girlfriend?

I expect you haven't. She was a vampire, you know, because the world is supernatural and amazing and everything ugly in it is people. Things ended with a tithe of lifeblood and a stake I drove personally through her very own heart, and I expect you realize now that my heart, my darling, my count became my ex-specter. She haunts my blood still. Rip in pieces, baby.

That makes no sense.

There's the bus.

Hidden on the ass end of a makeshift bridge, between two vast dead parking lots, there exists an oasis. It's a small clearing between weeds and a drought creek and some sickly trees that probably never felt like they belonged anywhere. There's a picnic table. Maybe *oasis* isn't the right word.

I sit on the table, resting my feet on the bench where I imagine a corporate misfit sits to eat his sad ham-and-cheese five noons a week. And now he'll have my shoe crap on his ass; the whole oasis is sullied.

I listen. I watch. The singing of insects. Small night things flickering. Plants wilting with neglect. A shifty Jace shivering.

A security guard slowly drives past in the parking lot, yellow lights flashing, not appearing to keep to whatever interval I bet is expected of her. All it would take is an easy twist of the neck to catch me, but I've always gotten the impression that security guards are deliberately bad at their jobs.

One night, not too long ago, I ran into a security guard who seemed more jittery than I was about encountering another being in the dark. I don't think he was all there. The first thing he said to me was thanking God that I was a human and, after a long pause, he suggested that I would really like vacationing in his home country of Jamaica, even though he was clearly Mexican. I fucked off so hard that I almost ran. I suppose that means he's actually quite good at his job.

Before coming here, I went to the café, as I have the five nights since I met her. Just for a short while, in case all my roaming and sleeping misses her coming back. But my step could defile the place and the moment so please keep this all under your hat.

Earlier, at work, Jorge called me his friend when he wanted me to move from in front of the big trash can. That was rather gracious of him. Jorge is a good man, with a wife who picks him up in a green car, and he deserves both. More, even. A greener car, a better friend than me, and maybe even a second wife.

Savannah, as she handed me the day's handful of wrinkled bills, invited me to meet her at a bar later to spend some of it on a drink. I wore my shirt with buttons and, when I finally caught her attention, the bartender looked at me with withering contempt, even though I did have the buttons. She must have seen? Rude.

Have you heard the one about the flirtatious bartender?

She was all over me but I didn't engage because I couldn't tell if she wanted my dick or just the tip.

I doctored the cheapest beer they had on tap for eighty-fucking-three minutes, scribbling slow spirals on a square napkin, front, back, unfolded and inverted. I tried to be thoroughly oblivious, as we well know that others seen will sooner or later see you. And, naturally, the longer I waited, the less I wanted to be seen.

I can't stand to sip, sip, sip in a noisy bar, and not be the noise. But I really tried, you know? I waited and waited and waited and waited, but it got to be too much. Too open. Too modern. Too bright. Too full of people with easy lives who conspire to uninvent me, in broad barlight, shameless, even proud, condoned, heartened. I hated them and hate them now, truly, for hating me.

Is this sickness? Mine or theirs? Is it poison or antidote that I shun people, their groups, their activity, their color and life and noise? Seeking the dark. A perversity, surely, but a romantic one, long past its bedtime, bending toward early dawn quixotism.

Look. I know what you're thinking.

It's not that I don't understand—it's just…

Well… You wouldn't get it. Besides, there's nothing there.

I left a dollar and the bar, keeping a low profile. Is that a crack about my height? What a God damn knee-slapper it must have been, for the watchful post-predatory vultures sipping scotch and gloating at my sepulture. Or did my lonely vigil and lonely retreat go entirely unseen by anyone, vigilant avian or otherwise?

Which is worse?

What the fuck am I talking about?

The security guard passes again, refusing to see, hear, speak me. The ever-watchful owl, with those big, big eyes, watches nothing at all. I guess she's too busy waiting for the clock to tick, "Go home."

Who needs her? Let her play at her power plays, where I sit around waiting like a chump and a fucking fool and she knows she's better than me because I'm the one stood up with buttons on my shirt. I don't need it. I don't need them to see me. I don't need them to hear me. I don't need them to speak, understand, or love me. Because I'm here, with the night.

The night loves me.

The night loves me, and not in the way of the beneficent God, omnipresent, omniloving, omnipreying, such that His wolfish amazing grace is placed in equal parts among and in every sheep in every flock and every shitty fucking thing that happens to me goes unacknowledged by the saw-, heard-, spoke-no-evil herd but accompanied still by a bitter, divine snigger behind an ineffable hand.

The night loves me, and not in the way of the mid-class hooker, affectionately punch carding every John, Dick, and Jason every time they book her, until loyalty point discounts and simple proximity slip into dangerous attachment, adjacent to feeling, leading first toward a smorgasbord of on-the-hotel orders and then to calls ignored, unexplored options, and cautious offing of what could have remained forever a strictly transactional passion.

The night loves me, and not in the way of the unicorn—charming, beautiful, everybody's darling—who can dig out the best in every horrid little pest and even in a stupid, quasi-gook loser to pull out of ruin for a few months until she scores someone better, then collects her severance, gets her revenge, and gently places him back where and how she found him, except now with the memory of a fragrance and meaning for a loss that before her had been nameless.

The night loves me, completely, unconditionally, in all her multiplexity with stars in her eyes, a fat black belly, and heavenly thighs. Her affections are comforting and protective, draped and wrapped around me in gossamer strands, preserving me in moonstruck glass to be treasured forever. She washes me clean, forgiving and rinsing away every deficiency and sin— there are so very many—and I am perfect, not in the eyes of any casual observer or even mine, but in her eyes. In her eyes, I am perfect. In her starry eyes, I am enough. In her starry fucking fuck-me eyes, I am here and seen and heard and real and wanted.

The night loves me... As pathetic as it is to depend on anyone or anything outside of my own self, she keeps me from crawling into a cave deep in my heart and hibernating through a winter that may never end. In a world that pollutes Heaven out of the Aether altogether, she's the only one to ever bring it back. She holds me coldly, a sheet of ice metal upon burning skin and soul, drawing out like toxins everything but a solace that doesn't defy but joys in the winter. Here, I am alone but not alone and she's here with me and I know she'll never go.

A place is only as real as my place in it, and nowhere and nothing else is as real as here, now, with her. Everything else, everyone else, in their continuous, unconscious betrayal of my being, perpetuate at my sufferance. That's all.

Have you heard the one about and out alone like a demented jackal yipping at a moonlit night that could never hear him?

"I hear you," she answers.

I pretend not to hear.

She invites me to spend the night with eyes wide and pleading. I refuse, for some reason I can't name. I want to say something but I've fallen voiceless. I think she has too.

She hugs me for a long time. I breathe in the faint scent of flowers and liquor.

I leave.

The night closes in.

It smells like the city is burning.

I'm stretched thin, out, pulled along after whatever will take me. I must be hollowed out entirely by now, singing with echoes inside that I wish I could at least hear.

I walk to the bus stop, slow, as slow as I can drag myself. I fear this is the only moment of peace I'll have today. Every step, every day, I feel closer to the edge of something. I'm scared to say what. I'm scared to see. I keep stepping. It follows me.

I take the back roads, where nobody walks and nobody drives. I don't want to be seen. I don't want to find myself tempted. I don't want to feel it. I don't want this thought in my temple.

Something restless and departed circles and circles in my chest. It brushes against the ribcage to remind me that it's still there. Breathless and remembering. Recollection centers me. Skies died, came to embers, and the cold wind leaves me trembling.

I don't notice at first what's happening outside, what's creeping up with an icy claw extended. A monster crawls out of a crack in the sidewalk, rises up, looms, hunches over me. It snarls. It retches. It calls me a slur but the wrong one, darling.

The stench of rot. Blackened teeth. A monstrous, monstrous bulk in wretched rags. It snarls. It retches. It's not supposed to be outside. It's not supposed to have flesh.

What does it want?

It's not supposed to be outside!

***

When nothing else is left, desolation keeps me company. It gives me form and identity, forms lack into entity. Pitiful, I know. From so many angles. But still.

I dreamed of your... Well, I don't know. Sometimes it's better not to be too sure what's going on in there, you know? *Do* you know?

The phone tells me, first, that I have three missed calls from Jorge and, second, that it's late in the afternoon, although the sun appears to be fast. Is the sky darkening prematurely or have I blackened my air and refused to notice? I swear, I used to know this...

Have you heard the one about the sleeping god and the fucking sun?

The joke doesn't really make sense, but it's not like you'll ever make it to the Helios Theater anyway.

I roll out of bed and fall the whole foot to the ground. I roll to a crouch, push up, wobble, push again, make it to my feet. Every movement is accompanied by a small, petulant groan from the floorboards and the fragile crepitation of my knees.

I shuffle to the door, along the way reorganizing the mess of my room into a slightly different mess. Laundry shifts from desk chair to bed, naturally. The lone slipper belongs in the opposite corner with the other lone slipper. Computer, turn on and then go back to sleep. Towel, you're with me. Everything in its place.

My place was missing for some time, and then I finally came home and placed myself in bed for some more time. All told, I apparently lost three days between dreaming, sleeping, and dreaming, although I wouldn't be able to with much reliability explain where they'd gone. Sometimes it's best not be too sure, if I can believe that.

Worlds are kept under lock and key. One way or another. Did you know that? It's right in front of us. Why do we never see it?

A wandering sleeplessness revealed to me a delirium that revealed to me a key that revealed to me a whole fucking world. As puzzle boxes go, this one was simple and brutal.

I slowly pull open the door, duck under my spider roommate's web, and creep down the stairs from my little attic room. At this time of day, at this time of week, any of my housemates could be skulking about. The trumpets and stomachache bass of an unambitious caped affair carry up from downstairs and mask the sounds of first my creaky footfalls and then the hissing of the shower.

I watch rivulets of grime stream into the drain until they decide to clean themselves up and run clear. The shampoo bottle says to wait a few minutes post-lathering to unleash the magic—their words—so I mold my hair into a mohawk, and then devil horns, and then the kind of slicked-back, briefcase-and-necktie hairstyle I'd expect the devil to actually have. Then the falling water washes it out, suds and styles and fancies all.

I stand for too long under the stream, long past the soap washing away and the wizening of my fingers. I try to remember where I went.

There are worlds hidden away in the wastelands too null and void for people to risk exploring, even wastes like me. Locks and keys, for good reason.

I think that I went there. I think that there were others. The middle of nowhere, the people under covers. Or am I thinking of a state of mind and no place at all? Locks? Keys?

Or, my God, have I been in hallucinations and bed the whole time, fever dreaming up bullshit and cobwebs, boring the spiders with my incoherent lock-and-key word salad?

Have you heard the one about the woman whose whole day got turned upside-down?

One fateful morning, this woman went out on a hike. It suddenly started pouring rain, and then, as she was rushing back to the trailhead, she was bitten by this huge, venomous spider. In the ambulance, she started hallucinating demons and monsters and all kinds of fucked up nightmares coming to get her. And, finally, to top it all off, she woke up in the hospital, still an Australian.

Is that racist? I hope so.

There's a banging on the door. It sounds assertive but calm, deliberately non-aggressive. What a knock. How long have I been in here?

I quickly finish up. As I hurry out of the bathroom in my towel, I almost run into one of my housemates, who's standing in front of the door, smiling with a backpack. She's petite, brown, tastefully made-up. Stunning, frankly. Sometimes I see her studying in the kitchen when I sneak out for food at unreasonable hours. She prevents me from picking at other people's snacks, but she does at least greet me by name even when we have nothing to say to each other.

Her mouth moves but it sounds like nothing I've ever heard.

I think I heard a door slam behind me. I think I heard myself. I think I heard the spiders whisper when I embraced finally that nagging derangement that's been tugging on my sleeve for my whole sad, fucking sad life.

I think I heard them say that I've become something else, some other species, many-legged and tiny, that doesn't, won't, can't talk to people. I've become voiceless, devoid of language, like the spiders—save for that mouthy cunt, Charlotte, I guess.

Break into the new world and the old one is closed off to you, as it turns out. Locks and fucking keys.

I shake the water out of my ears after staring at her for a long, confused moment. She laughs and repeats, "Hey, Jace! Sorry. I just need to brush before going to class."

"Oh," I say. "Sorry," I say. My voice is so small, like a spider's.

She tells me not to worry about it as she heads in. She says she'll see me later.

I return to my room without answering—because I'm not sure if she will—and sit naked at my dozing computer. I use one of eight legs to shake it awake, another to scratch my neck, a third and fourth to hold my head and lean on the crappy desk, and two more to steady its crappy wobbles.

Am I high? I don't think I took anything—I wouldn't.

Is she brushing teeth or hair? Or something else? I still don't know her name.

I still don't know what I thought has been happening all this time. Or what's actually been happening, for that matter.

Jesus Christ. What's happening to me? What's this world doing to me? Do you know? I ask my internet friends what I should have said to her, but they suggest only that I'm gay.

I should have left that key where it was.

"Emma," I rasp. I read somewhere—probably on *The Used Car Salesbro Blog*—that saying people's names makes them like you better. Extrapolating from that, it must be better still if your voice frays from disuse. I know these things. I could sell you a car, brother.

Emma casts a long, impenetrable shadow against the building behind her, stares into air, and punctuates my whole aphonic existence by pretending she never heard. She's sitting on a table in the cold blue-white light from the parking lot, with her feet upon attached bench and elbows upon attached knees and no cares upon shoulders, which may or may not be attached beneath an oversized, blue wooly sweater missing half a sleeve. Blue makes comfy sweaters. I know these things too.

It's been eleven nights since we last spoke. Three since I last spoke to anyone. One since I spoke aloud to the ghosts just to have spoken.

"Have you heard the one about the man who tried to invent a spoke-less bike?"

She slowly turns her head to look at me. Then says, "Sorry. Sometimes I don't hear so good. What did you say?"

"Uh… Have you heard the one about the guy who tried inventing the spoke-less bike?"

She keeps looking.

"He got nowhere—fast."

I think she still can't hear me.

I cough the cobwebs out of my throat before saying, "The lights here. You're the one who turns them off."

"Yep."

"Why?"

"I like it this way."

"The lights are pretty."

She nods slowly and looks away across the parking lot. I walk over and sit on the table next to her. She slides over a little to make room. That's a small sign of acceptance, I think. Right? I'm just glad she doesn't get up and walk away from me altogether. That's happened before.

Our thighs just slightly touch and she doesn't quite pull away and she's wearing shorts and that's her bare thigh there just slightly touching me. I think maybe she isn't a ghost, after all. And maybe she doesn't hate me. She looks down at our touching thighs for a moment but doesn't say anything. Do you think her legs are cold?

"How?" I ask her.

"Mm?"

"How do you turn off the lights?"

"Follow the wires, stupid."

Rude. "Oh," I say mildly. "So... You went to some places and now you're back here, huh?"

She smirks to herself. "You been waiting for me?"

"No," I say. I haven't been back *every* night.

"Mm."

"You don't believe me."

"Mm."

A silence falls between us. I need something witty to say, for once, lest she should come to her senses in the gaps. She breathes louder than I would have expected her to, with her pasty, scarecrow build.

Right as I feel I'm on the verge of starting a killer joke, she cuts me off. It's fine, though. There's something to be said about something being said to you at all.

"So, why do you come here, Jason?"

"Jace. I don't know. To be alone."

"Why would you want to be any more alone than you so obviously are?"

Well, first of all, fuck off. Second, "Because... Because everything ugly in the world is people. Why shouldn't I?"

"'Everything ugly in the world is people'," she repeats slowly. She grunts thoughtfully to herself. "Maybe you're onto something there. Is that why you've been here every night for two weeks? Keeping an eye out for some ugly people? Have you tried a mirror?"

She smirks to herself. One eyebrow twitches. Does she think I'm ugly?

"But I haven't." The truth is a little worse. But she couldn't know anything about it unless she were also here, prowling after me like a weirdo.

"Mm."

Silence. I don't try to come up with a joke. Maybe we can just be here together. Maybe something will happen. I sit, wait, listen.

"Listen," she says. I've *been* listening. "Jason. First, you should have acknowledged that awesome burn. It's, like, really not cool that you ignored it. Second—and this is the important one, so listen—this isn't your fairy tale, coming-of-age, feel-good, virgin-finally-gets-some-pussy story. Okay? You don't get the girl. I'm not here to save you. Okay? Let's just be cool and we can be friends. Okay?"

"Of course," I say. Have you heard bullshit like this? The unmitigated gall of her to tell lies like that... This *is* my story.

"Sure. Honestly, I don't see why you even felt the need to say that. And it's *Jace.*"

"I get people, alright? I get how they think. I know what you're thinking, even when you think you're being sly. It's sweet, and creepy, and sweet. And I just need us to be clear. And you shouldn't be mad. Okay?"

"Yeah. Definitely. Same page." Fuck you. I don't mean that. A tiny bit. I shouldn't be mad, I know. God knows I need friends. *A* friend. Well, aside from Jorge when I'm in front of the trash...

"Friends," I say. "You know what I'm thinking? What am I thinking, friend?"

"You come here to be alone, even though you're so *clearly* lonely. You get how stupid that is, on some level, but you've turned into this bitter little loser who hates the people he wishes would be his friends. You don't know how to talk to people and so they end up hurting you and you don't understand why. Because you're stupid. So, you come here to be alone and get even worse at talking to people and wish someone would come and save you. And you think someone *finally* has. But that's not why she's here. I'm not the one to save you. People just don't *do* shit like that. Also, you're stupid. That's the really important part. That should be the major takeaway: stupid."

I feel I ought to be allowed to be mad about that one. That's not fair, is it? Why *is* she here, then? What's *her* problem if she thinks she knows all of mine?

But I can't ruin this. As calmly as I can manage, I ask, "How do you figure all that?"

"I get people. Your suffering isn't as unique as it feels to you. Don't get all heated about it."

"I'm not getting heated about anything. Stop saying that. I just think—what if you're just wrong? Maybe you're projecting."

"Oh my *god*," she laughs. "No. You fucking dork. I've had lots of friends like you. Trust me. I *get* people."

I don't think she does. Not me, anyway. No one does. Not even you. Don't tell anyone I said that, especially not you.

After a long moment, I ask, "You have a lot of friends?"

"Some."

"Oh."

"Mm." She studies me for a second, and then continues, "Maybe I'll introduce you to them some day. Lord knows you need it."

I do. But I don't like being told that. I say nothing. We sit quietly for a long time, listening to all the night sounds that make up late night silence. I hear insects, distant traffic, wind, other insects, the creaking of sleeping construction sites.

My ass feels wet and slimy from the cold of the table. I hope it's not actually wet or slimy. I hope she doesn't abandon me after seeing the slimy, wet stain on my butt.

Have you heard the one about the perpetual junk wars of the slime people?

We must end this viscous recycle of violence.

That's pretty bad.

"Okay!" Emma exclaims. It startles me. I look at her, confused, reluctant to ask and be called stupid again.

She ignores me and pulls a phone out of some secret pocket. It's a newer one, the kind that's all screen and shows pictures. I lean slightly to snoop but can't make out what she's typing. She smells nice. The reply is almost immediate and she barely reads it before thumbing the screen dark and looking up to catch me mid-snoop.

"Let's go," she says, jumping up and marching off, not waiting to see if I actually follow. I do, obviously. What the Hell else am I supposed to do?

"Where?" I ask when I catch up.

"You can meet some of my friends."

"Some day?"

She doesn't answer.

"Fifty-six, by the way."

"Mm?"

"What I was thinking, when I asked... what I was thinking. It was the number, fifty-six." It wasn't.

"You were way off," I say. I don't think she gets it.

Emma leads me traipsing and trespassing through several corporate campuses, a parking garage, an empty industrial backroad. Clinging to their boundaries is the gaunt life that found its gaunt way.

We're a pair of urban jackals ourselves, prowling a world lost before we were ever born. We route through every liminal space, cracks and slipshod gaps between hulks of concrete and steel, around every globe of artificial light, long past where the alien palm trees give way to native weeds and gravel and dust. There's a kind of delicate, tail-wagging joy to these no-man's-lands. There are few, precious few places left these days for us no-man's-dogs.

She pauses, ears pricked, and gives me a look. I think it's a bewildered look, or questioning, or nervous. It's hard to tell with the yellow-green glow in her eyes. And quickly they flick away like a pair of fireflies. She continues on and I follow. We go to the dead end of a dark alley and through a narrow gap hidden behind a dumpster.

Emma's an entirely different color with each change in lighting, so pale of complexion that she barely has any color of her own. The sweater, however, stays more or less blue and more or less comfy. I suppose I change colors too, although I don't know how to look. I always look the same to me.

We travel along a dark stretch of abandoned railroad running between two near endless lines of factories. I can hear machinery and workers inside the square whitewashed buildings, even at this time of night, even at this place of nothing, even on both sides yet entirely unalike. They sound like ghosts. Their sleepy phantom voices mock us as we step blindly from sleeper to sleeper.

"What if someone's out here?" I ask Emma. My voice feels profane here. I'm tainting a perfect and perfectly desolate landscape just by being here. I expect the ghosts to scatter, but they go on with their distant chattering.

"There isn't."

"How do you know?"

The silhouette before me stops and turns. I almost walk into her, and there's a small, self-conscious thrill in that. I can just barely make out a weird look she gives me. "Don't you feel it?" she asks. "There's no one here."

I don't. I do. I don't know. I don't feel the psychic pressure of human weight like I sometimes do, or imagine I do, but that's nonsense because there she is, weighing and pressuring and being human. I want her to like me, so I agree, "Oh. Yeah. I guess you're right."

We continue walking the right of way. I try to be someone who belongs, here, with her, at minimum, but in general if I can.

After several minutes, Emma steps gingerly off the tracks toward one of the never-ending factories. We crunch over coarse gravel, climb onto a waist-high concrete platform, and push open a rusting metal door like any other. It squeals painfully but the ghosts are, naturally, dead to all pain, sound, and living intrusion.

We check our poltergeist escort at the door. They call to us wistful and gentle in their distant white noise voices.

Inside, there's a sound as if I'd walked into a room where everyone had just been talking about me, and not kindly, at that. What did I do? Why did the man sneer? I can feel the dark room staring at me in embarrassed, malign quiet.

Who's in here, staring at me like this? What if this is a trap?

If someone were to corner me right now, with knife in hand and no demands in particular, I'm not sure what I'd do. I'm not sure if I'd call for help. I wouldn't know how. I can't imagine what that would even sound like, what to do with my voice. I fear that nothing would come out, or that no one would come. What if no one comes for me? Who is there? I don't think I'd call for help.

You must think that's pretty damn funny, all things considered.

"Relax, Jason. It's fine," Emma says over her shoulder, without stopping.

It's Jace.

Someone's here. Here and not talking. I feel them. I don't. Someone's here. I resent their intrusion, and the fact that I'm the actual intruder here. I hope they don't hurt me.

Emma seems unperturbed. I follow her out of a narrow hallway into a large room populated by the bloated corpses of long abandoned industry.

There's a light ahead, and I shadow a silhouette against it.

Have you heard the one about the telegraphing dramaturge?

She puts a spotlight in each corner of the theater to highlight the tragedy's most important actors, so everyone knows what's going to happen when they see the four shadows.

Curtains close on that garbage joke. I come back and Emma's not where I left her. I jog to catch up right as she steps into the light.

Four old-fashioned table lamps in various states of disrepair are arranged in a rough square. They create a four-shadowed spotlight clearing between conveyer belts and bulbous tanks and rusted out metal monsters like I've never seen.

In the clearing are three people who silently watch us approach. They don't look like bulbous tanks and rusted out monsters, of course, but they have a way of blending in with the furniture, all the same. I guess this room is full of all manner of black pots and kettles.

"Hey, guys," Emma says. "Early, huh?"

They don't answer. There are two men and a woman.

"This is Jason," she says, gesturing vaguely at me. It almost sounds like she's asking.

They don't answer, except for a little, fluttery wave by the woman. Emma leads me into the spotlight. She spreads her arms in theatrical confusion, or disbelief, or pure, unadulterated showmanship. I don't know. Is this a show? Am I the star?

"Jace," I say. "Hi." I don't give them the chance to snub my handshake.

After a moment, the black guy says to Emma, "This isn't a halfway home for your sad losers."

Could've fooled me.

"Could've fooled me," Emma replies.

The woman giggles. I exhale sharply. No reaction from the men. The one who hasn't spoken is squatting on a milk crate and looks ready to never react to anything ever until the end of time. Maybe he'd laugh his ass off at Armageddon, at least.

I think that one's probably a werewolf. He's really big and hairy. I can just eyeball these things.

"Why are you like this?"

"Mm?"

"Get him the fuck out of here."

"Danny!"

"That's not very welcoming of you."

"People like him are better off not coming here."

"'People like him.'"

People like me?

"Oh, Emma, you know he didn't mean it like that."

"You don't have to drag every depressed shit you meet down with us."

"Oh, don't say it like *that*!"

"That's not nice. I think I'm dragging up here."

The other woman giggles at that.

I'm right here.

"Don't encourage her, Angela. He shouldn't be here!"

"Where, then?"

"*Anywhere*! Anywhere else!"

I'm right here.

"I don't think I mind being here…"

The wolfman sneezes or snarls into his sleeve.

"See?"

"Why can't you just leave well enough alone!?"

"Oh, Danny, you're getting worked up!"

"I mean, look at him. He *wasn't* well enough alone."

"*I'M NOT GETTING WORKED UP!*"

…I'm right here.

"Would *you* have left him alone?"

The definitely worked up Danny glares at me.

"I'm right here," I say.

"Oh, I know you wouldn't have, Danny. Not you. Never," the other woman, Angela, says.

"We help our brothers and sisters trapped out here on the edge. That's *you*, you dweeb," Emma says.

There's a long pause. The hard mask on Danny's face softens, just slightly.

"There he is," Emma says.

"Fuck you, Emmadora."

"Don't call me that."

He walks over and roughly shakes my hand. Luckily, he doesn't try to do one of those cool black guy handshakes with twelve steps—I only know the first three.

"Welcome to fucking nowhere," he says.

"*Good luck*," he says.

"I'm right here," I say.

Danny smiles in a mean way, like it's high school all over again and he can throw a spiral and I can't. I don't like him. He says, "Sure are, kid," before walking back to his place in the spotlight.

Wait. Emmadora?

"Emmadora?"

"Shut up."

Rude.

Emma—Emmadora—gets talking to Danny and Angela at the center of the lit area, stranding me at the penumbra.

After a minute, I start planning out how I might take the tiny shuffles and steps backward to edge myself out of this situation so I can Irish-Goodbye it and go home. But then the wolfman reaches back and tosses down another dusty milk crate with an almost hostile carelessness. He gestures for me to sit, so I do, because he is much bigger than me.

He slurs something brief, placing a massive, furry hand on his chest, of barrel nature, of course. Both his beard and demeanor are at least half-animal. His voice is deep as a coma but smooth and even faintly British, rather than the brutish, deep-woods growl I was expecting.

If you ask me, his inability to speak coherent English supports both my theories: that he's a werewolf and that he's British.

But no one asked me.

"Jace. Thanks," I say. He nods. I nod. He doesn't smile, so I don't. He barely even looks at me, so I don't look at him either. He's much, much bigger than me.

We sit without talking and watch the talkers. Emma(dora) and her friends have their friendly banter and discussions and debates, as friends do. Presumably. I'm not really listening.

Angela is shorter and wider than me and has a lot of piercings that make me uncomfortable to look at. I don't like her out-there glasses either, but she seems bubbly and sweet, maybe a little carbonated. It makes me think that she must not be very bright, but that's the kind of unkind thing people think about me.

Danny is tall and athletic and looks like he's prom king of the group, even though the wolfman is still bigger. His hair is almost not there. I don't know why black guys do that sometimes. He makes everyone laugh when he talks, even though he was mean to me before.

Emma is long and pale and smiles with her big mouth when she talks to her friends with her one sleeve missing and her name is really Emmadora but she doesn't like to be called that. Occasionally, she looks over to check on me, maybe offers an encouraging grin, or waggles her eyebrows to broadcast some secret message I don't have an antenna for. And then she goes back to pretending I don't exist.

I sneak a look at the monster next to me to see what I should be doing but he's just looking at the floor. I'm not sure if he sees it. That doesn't seem like the socially appropriate thing to do in this situation, but I may give it a shot anyway.

Soon, others begin to trickle in, in their ones and twos and even one three, but mostly ones. Every time the squeal of the door echoes through the place, the buzz of conversation halts as people watch to see who's coming in. It's almost like when guests are announced at those fancy, old-timey galas you see in the silvery films of Pedowood.

Some of the revelers hang around, breaking off into clusters throughout the room, scattered among the relics in a pattern that I think implies a good deal of shady commerce. Angela, social butterfly that she apparently is, flutters from one group to another, laughing and smiling like she's actually having a good time.

Altogether, I think I count almost two dozen people passing through, but I'm not great at math. Is that a lot for this kind of party?

They come in an absurd array of sizes and shapes and colors, but most of the newcomers are uniformed to try for the title of King of Hobos. I think some of them literally are. Homeless, I mean. Not necessarily kings, but who can say? I know I recognize one for sure from the shelter. He doesn't seem to notice me.

Most of them talk and chuckle and sometimes share or exchange drinks or money or bags of crap that could be anything, maybe even drinks or money. Probably just drugs.

For some reason, Angela appears to be involved in most of the exchanges. Her doughy little fingers move with surprising alacrity when there's dough involved. At one point, she catches me catching her leaning to peek into a man's bag when he's not paying attention. She laughs silently and holds a finger to her lips. I think we have an inside joke now, the two of us, but I don't get it.

Have you heard the one about the peeping fatso?

Please explain it to me if you have.

Sometimes individuals split off of one cluster and merge into another, but no one ever stands alone for long. Except for the wolfman and me, but we'd at least be alone together if he were actually present.

Everyone else bustles about, lively and friendly and together. Some don't seem to talk ever, but they make the rounds nonetheless. The funny thing, though, the thing you wouldn't notice except as an outsider looking in, is how they all look slightly lost or alarmed whenever they're between groups, as if they're not sure when they leave one group if they'll ever find another. This, I think, is the one thing that's common between all of them, no matter how they vary in every other way.

I've never seen such a diverse group of forgotten nobodies, all huddled together, as if, deep down, on some sad, hopeful, desperate, fucking stupid level, they're all thinking mere propinquity could turn a knot of perennial anomics into a community. But, I guess, what else is there to do but hope, and huddle, and playact, and hope?

It's funny, really. Don't you think so? I think so. It's comedy on a cosmic scale, a joke only God Himself could have come up with: derelicts, failures to integrate into any society offered to them, huddling together in a grotesque imitation of their own, until the joke finally stops being funny.

But I can't imagine such a joke ever will.

I smother a laugh, snort. I check if the wolf's watching me but he's tuned into another plane of existence altogether. It looks like no one's noticed at all, except possibly one silent bum glaring in my general direction with unfocused eyes. He could be staring at anything—likely two or three things at once—but I should be more careful.

I try not to giggle to myself at something no one else seems to see. It's a secret kind of joke, subtle to the point of vanishing, as is His way. The Divine Cipher. Who would've expected it to be a joke? I think maybe *that's* the joke.

Have you heard it, though?

Don't worry about it. You wouldn't get it. Besides, as jokes go, there's nothing there.

I snap back from the patch of floor I was laughing at when a small brown woman, smaller brown child in tow, appears suddenly before me. I look up and find that she's talking to someone else, and they've positioned themselves just in front of me, too close for me to not be involved but somehow not involving me anyway. The wolf is still there beside me, and he still appears not to have noticed.

The smaller brown child glances at me from time to time as she quietly eats a hot dog and walks a slow orbit around us. She kicks whatever pebbles or bits of debris she finds.

Is it a sin to bring an innocent to a place like this? More importantly, where are they passing out hot dogs? Are they free?

Another stranger joins the conversation and people shift in a way that makes me a part of the circle now. This is a little worse than before. I immediately zone out but watch the current speaker and nod slightly whenever someone makes eye contact.

Have you heard the one about the Chinese tourists in New York?

A couple of tourists from Wuhan are visiting the City of Apples and decide to try out the official state sport, hot dogs. They get their greasy bags from a greasy New Yorker at a cart and go sit on a greasy park bench to eat. After looking in his bag, one of the tourists asks his countryman, "Which part of the dog did you get?"

The small brown woman looks at me and says something. I nod politely and then have a tiny spasm as I return to consciousness.

Shit. What did she say?

"Great, Carla! How've you and little Isabel been doing?"

I don't know when Emma snuck up to sit next to me. She's sitting on the floor, getting all kinds of crap onto her bare legs, I'm sure. She smiles sardonically at me. What does that mean?

Danny, Angela, and a third homeless old man I don't know join the conversation, which grows the group to the point where I don't even have to pretend to pay attention anymore. Perfect. They get happy and boisterous as they debate some dumb thing or other. Danny makes everyone laugh.

Emma nudges me, pauses to wince when the group roars with laughter, then whispers, "You okay?"

"I'm fine."

"You sure? I'm just asking because you've been sitting here being an autist and growing roots all night."

"I'm *not* autistic."

"Oh, honey..." She smirks, raises an eyebrow for a moment.

"I'm not fucking autistic," I spit, with acid in my throat.

Emma blinks.

"I'm fucking sick of explaining myself over and over *and over again* to people from the *start*. And then they fuck off and there's another, and another, just the fucking same. They say, 'Jason—"

"Jace, calm down."

"—I don't follow. You—you're not making *sense*, Jason.' They say, 'You have *mental problems*, Jason. You'll have to do it *again*, Jason.' They call me *Jason* and *autistic* and...f-fucking crazy because they want—"

"Jace, please."

"—to make it *my* fault—m-my fault that they don't understand. I drag myself through this shitty fucking broken glass world that says it's *my* fault I'm all cut up, like I—like I *owe* them something. They owe *me*! They owe *me* an unpayable debt, not the other way around. The world owes—"

Emma puts a hand on my forearm and gives it a squeeze. She digs her nails lightly into the skin.

Shit. I glance up to find that the others are focused on their own conversations, or pretending to be out of vile politeness. Emma looks concerned, or embarrassed, or sad, or hungry. I can't tell what that look means.

Next to her, the rock-kicking little girl is staring at me, chewing thoughtfully. She raises her arm and offers me half a hot dog. She offers me her food, with her many-times-handed-her-down clothes and shoes that don't even fucking light up. She's a child, here, in this awful place, trying to gift me half a hot dog. I might cry.

"N-no," I say. "Not you. K-keep it."

The child returns to her meandering after a good, long, innocently soul-piercing stare.

Emma suggests we head out. I can feel her pity, her embarrassment. Jesus. I fucked up. Again. She'll toss me away in the gutter like yesterday's hot dog and I'll never see her again. And I'll deserve it.

The silent fucking bum is still glaring at something on either side of me.

"You have fun?" Emma asks, looking down to watch her footing on the tracks.

The buildings, white and haunted, pass slowly on either side.

"I'm not really the fun-having type."

"Yeah, I noticed…"

Fuck. "Sorry. Sorry I made you leave early."

"It was getting too loud for me anyway. You okay?"

"I'm fine."

"Say you're okay."

"I'm okay."

"Would you tell me if you weren't?"

"Yes." No.

"Okay." After a moment, Emma continues, "You seemed to get on with Sebastian, at least."

"Who?"

"The huge guy you were sitting next to all night? Are you serious?"

"Oh. I didn't catch his name." *Sebastian*? That's an incredibly wolfish name.

"Your only friend all night and you didn't even remember his name. Talk about rude."

"Well, he didn't actually *talk* to me or anything. I just sat where he put the thing so he wouldn't hurt me."

She laughs. "He wouldn't do that. I don't think so."

"He's a very large man."

"Yes, he is very large. But I don't think he'd kick your ass for not sitting."

"I think he was *super* high."

This is something that I expect Emma to laugh at but she doesn't. She sounds nervous when she says, "Yeah... I don't know if it's right that Angela does that but..."

"Angela does what?"

She sounds even more uncomfortable. "Look. Sebastian's an addict. Okay? Not great; it's just how it is.

"I tried to help but he *really* does not want it. He got kind of nasty, honestly. What can I do when he doesn't want to be helped? I *tried*. Okay?"

"I'm not—you tried. That's all you can do. It's not your responsibility. But what does Angela have to do with it?"

"He buys from Angela. It's safer than other shit he could be on. And better from someone he can trust than a stranger. Except…"

She looks at me, asking without asking if she should continue. I don't know how to answer without answering. She continues: "Except… Well, she told me once that she makes it stronger for him. Without… without saying anything. I don't think I've seen him even close to sober."

"Oh… Why? Is that legal? What if he overdoses?"

Emma takes a long time to answer. She doesn't look happy when I sneak a glance at her face. "I don't know. She says it's just to be safe. It's not like he's complaining. Okay? If not here, he'd be getting just as fucked up somewhere else, on something more dangerous… But I don't like it. It's not right that she does that but—you know what? A part of me kind of gets it."

"What? Is he dangerous? I think he's a werewolf."

She chuckles. "Jackass," she says softly.

I fake a laugh so she thinks I was joking.

"Sometimes," she continues, "things seem kind of *off* with him, you know? He seems kind of… mixed up."

"Mixed up how?"

"Well, he's a drug addict, isn't he?"

"But that's not what you meant."

"We-ell... I think he's still deciding if he likes us. Maybe he wouldn't hang around with us if Angela wasn't his dealer. Maybe he thinks, like, we're beneath him."

"Well, he is very, very large."

She laughs and agrees that, yes, he is very large.

"But that doesn't really explain the thing with the drugs, unless *off* means *school shooter* in your world. Do you think he'd actually hurt us if Angela weren't doping him?"

"I don't think so."

"You don't sound convinced."

"Look. Sebastian's just a snobby junkie. He likes getting high and thinking he's better than everyone, and Angela helps him with that. That's it. He's not some big, bad wolf. So, you can drop it, okay? He's a nice guy."

She still doesn't sound convinced. But I want her to stick around so I drop it. I say, "He was nicer than Danny, at least."

"Don't worry about Danny. I know he sounds like a big asshole but he's actually a really good guy, I promise."

I shrug. After a few seconds, I remember that she's not looking at me and say, "I guess. I mean, you *did* hug him when we left..."

This time, she looks at me, and then trips, curses, stops, and looks at me.

"What's your point, Jason?"

"Jace."

"Fuck! What's your point, *Jace*?"

"Thank you. No point. Just an observation."

With the way the inhospitable lighting here hits her face, I can't make out her expression behind the panda bear shadow mask, but I can tell that it's changing. Damn it.

"Jace... Fuck!" She stutters and gestures wildly for a few seconds, and then says, "We *just* talked about this, Jace! Listen. I'm not trying to be a bitch, but you need to drop this. Okay? It's not going to happen. Don't get lost in your sad boy fantasies. Okay?"

Shit. "Shit. Sorry. I didn't mean anything. I just thought, you know, of course you're going to defend your boyfriend."

"Oh my god. Gross. He's not my *boyfriend*, stupid. Danny's my *brother*."

"Oh," I say. Good, I think. "But you don't look..."

"*What?*"

"You know...You're white and he's..." She knows.

"Black," Emma snaps. "He's my half-brother. And I'm *not* white. I'm Cuban."

"Cuban? Really?" Not Mexican? Not white? Have you seen her glow in the dark?

She looks annoyed.

"How'd *that* happen?" I ask. Emma turns and continues walking down the tracks without waiting for me. What the fuck did I do this time?

I catch up and say nothing.

Eventually, without looking up, she says, "We came over on a stolen boat when I was a baby; the government let us stay because of my fucked-up ears; my egg donor got hooked on heroin and overdosed like a fucking asshole; Pa met Mom; they had Danny; he was an arrogant little shit; still is; then, one day, Mom and Pa got sideswiped by a truck on the freeway because Californians can't fucking drive for shit and hate seeing a spic living a happy life."

"Jesus Christ," I say. "Sorry. You didn't have to—I meant, how are you a non-Mexican Hispanic in San Diego..."

"That's racist. Pa moved us out here for work. And then bounced."

"Oh."

"Off the pavement."

Jesus Christ. "Sorry."

We walk.

The thing she said about her... About the overdose. And Sebastian. I know, I know. That's not the sort of thing you say out loud. I look at Emma and she's watching me think it and I try to hold a poker face but I think she can tell.

She spits, "Fuck you, man," even though I didn't say anything. But maybe it *was* out of line, what I thought.

We walk.

"I'm sorry," Emma says eventually. "I was in—I shouldn't—let's just drop it, okay?"

"Yeah. Sorry. Dropped. Sorry." I try to tally the gaffes to make sure I covered everything. Two? Three? Just in case, "Sorry."

We walk.

"I'm from Chicagoland," I offer.

"What?"

"I—uh. I moved here from Illinois."

"Oh." After a long pause, Emma asks, "How'd that happen?"

"I took a bus."

She chuckles but doesn't respond otherwise.

"So, you're a Cuban raft baby?"

"Don't call me that."

"Sorry."

We fall into silence yet again. We walk. I light up and puff, puff, puff as we go. Emma gives it a look in my hand but says nothing. Her phone in its secret pocket buzzes once, twice, then falls silent. She doesn't check it.

Have I been here before? Well, yes. Duh. It looks exactly the same back-to-front. But otherwise?

There are food wrappers and empty bottles. There are grimy foam pads laid out in cozy corners. There are graffiti tags and murals and absolute masterpieces, all in alien tongues, all translating and reducing down to a plaintive, "I was here," that no living soul ought ever to see. We pass a couple of orphaned train cars, abandoned to rot like so many places and people and locks and—shit.

"Is Emmadora a Cuban name?" I find, when I look at her to ask, that she's already staring at me, but not in a way that seems good.

She takes a beat to answer. "Emma. And—"

"Sorry."

"—I don't know. Cubans love long, crazy names. But Pa was a dweeb, so maybe he just got it from some fantasy novel. I'm just thankful I don't have an apostrophe and three dashes in my name."

"Do Spanish names usually have a lot of those? How many dashes are in *Jorge*?"

"Shut up," she says, rolling her eyes.

Bitch.

"Do you speak Spanish?"

"Claro que si, comemierda."

"I can't tell if that actually means anything." She probably insulted me.

Emma giggles to herself and then, after a pause, asks, "Do you speak... uh. Asian?"

"I'm Korean. Half. And, no, you racist, I don't speak *Asian*." To the deep disappointment of all Koreans everywhere.

"Well, that's boring," she says. *She's* boring.

"Growing up, I thought I could be both, but it turns out I'm neither."

"What?"

Because I'm half-neither. But she wouldn't get it. I say, "Never mind."

We walk for a long time without speaking and eventually emerge from Ghost Factory Row onto a street with too many lanes for the no traffic on it. We stop and look at each other, then elsewhere, then each other again.

"Well," Emma says, slapping my arm lightly. "I'll see you around."

I'll never see her again.

Before she gets too far, I ask, "When?"

She spins to face me but keeps right on leaving, retreating backward into the darkness. "Around!"

Emma grins a big, squinty, toothy grin for a few more steps and then turns around and strides away. I stay where I am, watching her go. She's yellow-white beneath the streetlights and invisible between them, and eventually she leaves one and never reappears.

Not once does she look back.

Six hours since we last spoke. Five and a quarter since I got home. How many elevens of nights before we speak again?

I haven't slept. I sit in the cold blue dark and stare at funny videos on the computer. Sometimes I laugh. Sometimes I let them loop. My internet friends say I'll never see her again, and also that I made her up, and also that I might be black.

Have you heard the one about children and the dumbest timeline?

If you hit the hay early in December, the fat man and all his glorious morning gifts arrive earlier. Children believe that, because they're dumb.

Time doesn't really work that way, of course, but of course it really does, and there's no punchline and there's no time like the present.

Heh. Stupid kids.

If I don't sleep, tomorrow won't come, nor ten more nights, nor however many elevens more. The little ones know this.

At some point, that eagerness for each upcoming day ages out of us, and the void is filled with a shallow dread. Why hasten the next daybreak when the dawn brings only heartache? Isn't that why we're up all night? Isn't that sick? Nobody needs to be told that staying up all night is bad for you, but we never talk about the dangers of waking up.

But, of course, the space rocks spin heedless, in an act of personal disrespect that I personally find exhausting. I hear the delighted chatter of the early birds unwrapping their gifts. I taste the poison clinging to the fringes of the globe's fat pirouette.

I won't let the daylight sneak up on me now. I'm going to sleep.

I'm tired.

The water steams faintly. On it float enough sudsbergs to hide the flesh, bone, skin, soul, unpainted, lined with battle scars, flushed to ironic clay.

The bottles hang around like little spilled tankers. It's as yet unclear if there will be any ecological impact. Fingers would cross if they could.

I've buried myself to my tilted chin, so as to not see or be seen. Down here, where everything is supposed to be pressure, dark, terror, there is no pressure, no dark, no terror. No expectation, no disappointment. No thing here. Definition is and has always been pointless; I think I'm sure of that now.

My timeline is warped. It blurs and slows and completely no-call-no-shows for immeasurable periods. At one point, I was near scalding. Now? I don't know where now is. Cold, colder.

I can't remember.

I'm tired.

I wait. I drowse. I'm enormous now. I am tectonic. The tides lap against my sides and I am power, maybe dormant, maybe utterly world-destroying. But I am power, finally.

Rogue submarines nuzzle my slopes. They beg to be gathered up into my wake, shined, mounted, triumphantly taken.

What are trophies to a titan? I've had enough already. What? No.

I need to check. I need to measure them, measure up, measure down, measure, measure. I need to call. I reach out of the bath for my phone but the oceans are so heavy. It's not worth the titanic struggle, the flesh breathes to me. Slow. Heavy.

Vision smears and blurs, refusing my pleas for focus, focus, please! Sea monsters roar in my ears. I shout back but no one, no one ever hears.

I have to get up. I have to leave this world. It was a mistake to come here. I have to get up. I push off for a breach but the bone falters, topples, slumps and comes to nothing.

Tired.

I descend whimpering into my own depths. Deep, deeper. I've diminished into yet another wreck. Surd, voiceless cries. Down, down, down, I sink. Waves tease my eyes; I can't convince them to wince...

They'd wince to witness it. Or they'd laugh, gloat over how I've stumbled. I can't be seen like this. Not like this. Not here. I can't be seen to crumble.

Tired...

Light without heat, then bubbling twilight, and then no light at all. All gone. The hadal waters gurgle, echo, in my head, or what remains. I can't be sure, and I'm so fucking tired.

How far have I...? The skin, soaked through, withered... The skin, it registers cold, or numb, or pure, purest nothing. Maybe better this way. Imagine butterflying out... Having to wear it. How far...?

I forget now.

I forget...

Tired...

If I were a praying man, I guess I'd call on God to bless the winters and the falls for arranging tilts and orbits, just so, such that all the day's glory is packed into one compact block of hours for me to sleep through. Or, perhaps, He ought to gift Himself a fruit basket for putting together such a lovely seasonal arrangement.

I couldn't possibly know. He does work in mysterious ways, after all.

Have you heard the one about the praying man?

He prayed to God to win the lottery and finally climb out of the Hell that was his life of poverty. He waited and waited, for week after week, and month after month, but it just never happened. Finally, at the end of his rope, he cried out to the Heavens, "Why, God? Why won't you help me?"

And, lo, God's thundering voice came down to him: "Bro, buy a lottery ticket."

Sometimes I do actually wish I were a praying man, complete with all the false promises and hypocrisies and hopes. That's the key. Hope.

I suppose it ought to bother me that I cannot hope, but I suppose just as well it saves me the disappointment of being less…

Bullshit. I *wish*.

Whatever sour notes I may sing, we both know that I'm still sitting here hoping, and the disappointment swings and circles back around like a scorpion's sting. And, so, reflexive double agent that I am, I hope to not, so that I can romantically lament the absence of enchantment with the dark satisfaction of never having it dispelled.

What?

If I were a praying mantis, I would eat God's head.

Somehow, that's less dumb.

It's a disease of the psyche, truly, this hope business. Infectious and ravaging, it takes the best of us and empties them out utterly. I've seen the greatest people—much better than me, for sure—wrecked and left hollow. But here I am still, at once knowing and hoping, right and wrong, with all sides down.

As a silver lining, at least, that means I'm at a peak. I can see my house from here.

I've heard it said, by people who've never had a day an ice cream sundae couldn't fix, that going out into the world expecting, delivers. I don't pretend to understand the cranes and their supply lines, but that sounds to me like a hopeful rationalization for being wrong all the time.

But I *would* like an ice cream sundae right now. It could really fix this day I've been having. And my day has barely even begun.

I'm in bed still. I dreamed I fell back asleep in a great porcelain ocean and… I forget now. I forget a lot. I forgot to get out of bed. Time keeps marching, but it feels like I'm in slow-motion.

A day since I last ate; the meat grumbles but without the urgency that might drive me to hurry up and wait until the deadest hours so I can sneak out to steal oatmeal cookies from the housemates that I never see. Four days since I've gotten out of bed for any meaningful amount of time at all.

I walked by the abandoned railroad one night. It was the simple, no-frills walk of a boy with somewhere to be—though I, of course, have no somewhere to be ever.

I had to play it cool, you understand. I tossed only a disinterested glance down the tracks, for but a moment before continuing on.

Five days since I last showered. I don't smell it but I bet you would, with that famous nose of yours.

Two months since I last paid rent. I'm good for the money—as good as I can be for anything—but they haven't asked. They haven't knocked on my attic door. They haven't been to the top of this world at all, where I planted my lonely old flag some time ago and laid low.

I wandered nonchalantly along the railroad once, trying to reconstruct the treasure map out of what few landmarks there were the last time. Dead railroad cars, unique piles of trash, a million ghost factories, each sporting its own unique mural of nuclear shadow ghost graffiti. Those poor, blurry jap babies. If only someone could have remembered them.

I saw no treasure, and saw no need to be seen looking, so I turned back and didn't come back. Why can't I find that fucking *X*?

Searching online didn't work either, since I couldn't think of any distinguishing feature to pick it out of the satellite view lineup. And none of the internet strangers wanted to help. Although they did send me a bunch of pornos I didn't ask for.

Six days since I've been to work. Six days since I fucked off, on account of being told to fuck off, on account of it having been three days since I'd gone to work. "Fuck off, Jason," Savannah said, exactly. I didn't argue.

Even as I tossed myself out, never to be seen again, Anne Frank still never looked up from her diary, not with the one eye or the other. Is it too much to ask to have my existence acknowledged by *someone*? Maybe it would teach her a lesson if I told Hitler to check the attic.

Have you heard the one about my cross-eyed ex-girlfriend?

I dumped her because she was seeing someone else on the side. And because she was Jewish.

The really weird thing about it, though, is that Savannah told me to tell Jorge that he's fired too. Because he, allegedly, pulled a Jace and ghosted for a couple of days in a row, which is not like him. It's not like him at all, not with a car as green as his.

When she enlisted me to pass along the message, I genuinely thought she'd mixed us up, in some bizarre, color-blind act of post-racism, to confuse me for the responsible one.

Very strange. Possibly something I should be more concerned about. I should text him, or call, or organize a search party. I should do something. But my mind keeps going back to how Savannah first stood me up at that bar with all the buzzards, and now, with poor Jorge dragged along behind me, it's just, "Fuck off, Jason."

Four days since I could first examine how much that stung. Two since I could care.

It's Jace, by the way. You *do* remember that, right?

I went hunting a third time. It was a stakeout. I should have been looking for Jorge, but, then, do you think he would look for me? No one would. But would he?

I lurked sphinxlike for hours on the bus stop bench across the street from Ghost Factory Row. Unspeaking and perfectly still, save for the occasional flick of ear or tail, I watched with my shining eyes the comings and goings of absolutely no one, save for a lone, orange cat.

He stopped and warned me, one alley cat to another, of danger and moonlight and iron man-things, before vanishing into a shadow. Orange makes kindhearted cats, I guess. Too bad I'm not more orange myself.

The iron man-things came and went. Sometimes—not always—the buses slowed for me and tried to stare down my sphinx eyes before giving up and moving on.

The times they didn't slow for me, I couldn't tell if they failed to see me or if I'd done some subtle thing right or wrong that caused them to roar past. Just pass me by, brother. I'm not going anywhere.

Two hours since my housemate killed herself, I'd guess. In the bathroom, I'd guess. With pills, I'd guess. I doubt I could tell you where those guesses are coming from. Why bother?

A little over an hour since I heard screaming, and the red and blue lights paint my walls still.

She was studious. She was beautiful. She brushed something before going to class. She saw me when I was around to be seen and greeted me by name, even when there was no name to be greeted. I never learned hers. And now she's gone and offed herself.

Have you heard the one about the broken brother?

Paul said to his brother, "I can't take this anymore."

Paul said to his brother, "I don't want to be alive."

Paul said to his brother, "I wish I was dead," but then he fought like Hell when a fucked-up druggie turned mugger turned murderer.

Don't get offended now. Believe me, I know that it's horrific, tragic, fucked up, all the bad things, sure, sure...

But it's also a little funny, in a devastating sort of way. Don't you think so? Poor, suicidal Paul and his new knife, intertwined like Romeo and Joliet on the shitty city sidewalk, with broken knuckles and junkie blood under his nails.

What did you really want, man? Tell us how you really feel.

Sorry. That's disrespectful, isn't it? No disrespect meant, of course, Paulie Baby. Rip in pieces.

I know, I know. I can say I mean no disrespect, but then, you wonder, what *did* I mean?

There are some thoughts that are best left unvoiced, I *know*. We leave the ideas nebulous, things that are felt, experienced, intuited by almost everyone and never collapsed into a thought, into words, into something that can be shared with others.

There must be good reason for it; there must be some safety in keeping it an open secret from each other and ourselves. Surely, it must be the wise choice, simply on the basis of consensus. There *must* be some justification for keeping ourselves alone in this. Maybe I don't entirely understand, but I can understand that everyone else does.

I could just not think about it. I could just ignore it like I'm supposed to. I could go back to drifting languidly through a haze of sensations and soft-hammer-to-knee-jerk reflexes. It comes easily enough to me, so easily that I'll go without realizing for days, weeks, making my circuits in the emotional state machine, from one node to the next, surviving and moving as triggered by external stimuli, like the automaton that I am.

I could do this. But, if I do, how will I talk to you?

Are you even paying attention? Are you there?

I worry sometimes when I realize suddenly how many days it's been since I last checked. Weeks or months, a whole lifetime, evaporated right under my nose. I don't want you to miss out on anything, but it's so easy to forget.

Is my attention holding you here or is it the other way around? Are you paying attention at all? Is that even the right question? Or do I talk, talk, talk, lay one desperate word after another in eternal procession, simply to avoid having to face what's happening around me right now?

I ought to at least look out the window. If anyone's out there looking up, it would prove that I'm alive, and offer the corollary that I'm humane enough to at least rubber my neck.

No. Human. What's humane about gawking? The saintly spine spins not, God always says. Probably. It's been some time since I've cracked open a Bible. But maybe even "human" is a title I've fallen short of. Would you be able to tell? Would you tell me?

The window's open. I leave my window open always, unless it rains, which happens for one week a year and is dark and lovely in its way. I hear the murmurs below of grim professionals handling a run-of-the-mill calamity.

The lights spin, red and blue, blue and red.

"The fifth tonight," I imagine a cop saying, fat and bored and coated head-to-toe in powdered sugar.

Heads and hearts turn as someone out and down there starts wailing. The loss takes a piece of us, but that thievery of grief is what reunites us with the lost. I tell myself this. I don't tell the wailer.

The lights spin, blue and red, red and blue.

I ought to look. I ought to at least do that much. If I were a good person—if I were a person at all—I would drag myself over and forward and up, one foot in each direction, to the cracked sill and open air, and I would at least acknowledge that this person existed in my world and suffered in my world and maybe fought like Hell when the pills and bathwater—I'd guess—turned murderer in my world.

I stay where I am. I stay what I am.

Things go quiet, mournful. It's a hypnotizing time, this morose aftermath. The air is heavy. A car door. Low voices. A light wind. The muted noises blur together. The lights spin, blue and red, and so on.

The shadows twist and dance on my walls, beckoning. But I don't intend to join that grim conga line with the Paulie Babies and What's-her-names of the world. No disrespect, of course. It's just not my scene.

I ought to at least look. I ought to say something. What could I say? What eulogy can I offer when I don't truly know anyone? If I were a good person, I'd find something, make up something. I'd say something nice and solemn and deep as her despair probably was. I'd at least say something...

Time slips around and through me and runs off into the night. With it go ambulances and police cruisers and all the rest, until there's only me and my quiet black world and this sad, shocked house of sad, shocked people.

I would have expected the housepeople to at least come up and knock, to at least check in and inform and give a little knock. She would have. I would not have.

They don't even want the rent. It's an entirely new level of not giving a shit.

I light a cigarette. There are rules against doing this in the house, but no one will stop me. They didn't even come up for a literal life-or-death.

The orange glow doesn't penetrate the darkness nearly as well as the reds and blues did. I take a drag, hold it, and exhale a shadowed plume.

Here we all are, in the sleepy home where someone just died, and they don't bother to tell me about it, or check if I've been pilled, drowned, and dead all this time. They don't even check if I'm huffing and puffing lung cancer into the paint, knowing full well that I won't be paying that fine.

They don't even check on me. Maybe they'd be glad to finally be rid of me.

"*Are* you alive, then?" the bloody-handed bath bubbles up to me, hushed and secretive after routing through all the piping between us.

"Are you okay?" the water breathes, like I should have, like I didn't, because everything is a joke.

"Are you alive?"

This isn't what I wanted.

The veins of this town teem with a life that feels huge and metropolitan and wasted and frighteningly vibrant. There's too much in too little. It's too disordered, too full. Full of children, delving for a laugh, tipsy and tipping this way and that.

Below, an imperfect circulation of shadows. The warm subterranean passages web from building to building, quad to quad, serving at one point, the legend goes, as snow bypasses and now as simply null spaces, loose casings of pipes and spider webs and forgotten freight.

And me.

And us. Here we are.

Flashlight in hand, I duck beneath pipes, clamber over clutter, wipe the eons of dust from my expensive jeans. He lopes behind me, leaps laughing over obstacles, disappears up ahead and lounges in the dark waiting for me to catch up.

His long, graceful limbs, effortless athleticism, undisguised showboating… It's irritating.

I can't believe he's here with *me*. No one has ever been so lucky.

I look behind me but everything vanishes into shadow beyond the weak cone of my light. How far have we walked down here? It's been hours, surely. We must be well off campus by now.

I ask him and he smiles, shrugs, laughs. "What does it matter?" he says. Well, it does matter, I think. But I don't say so. He smiles, laughs, kisses me and runs off ahead to show off his agility. I can't help but smile after him.

When I catch up, I find him slouched at the edge of a square hole that completely takes up the dozen feet from wall to wall. His legs dangle carelessly into the void. I inch carefully up to peer into the pit, but it plummets well past the reach of my light. I look up and there's a mirror image, a column of shadow extending upward into the distance.

"What is this?" I ask.

"What does it matter?"

"Sometimes things matter!"

He whacks the backs of my legs and I crumple, fall—I cry out—and I'm caught in his arms. He cradles me against his chest. I want to hit him. I hang fiercely onto his neck. I think I might be crying. But he looks down at me, into my eyes, and he's smiling, and I can't help but smile back.

"Don't do that, asshole!"

He laughs. "But I caught you!"

"What if you didn't?"

"I would never let you fall."

"You could've missed!"

"I would *never*."

I know he absolutely means it but, still, there's this gaping hole pawing at my back and I can feel it there and I don't want to see it. I bury my head and into his chest ask, "Please, can we get up?"

"Of course, babe." He carefully sets me down next to him, leaps to his feet, and helps me up and away from the brink. I wrap my arms around him to settle my heart. He gently strokes my hair, for as long as I need.

Eventually, I step back.

"Better?" he asks.

"Better."

We share a smile, that secret grin we have, passing back and forth when no one's looking. Then he turns, runs at the edge, and leaps clear across the pit. I can't even get a word out before he's on the far side, smiling and waving at me like a maniac.

He beckons for me to come after him. "Come on! Jump!" he says, with that damned smile, that smile that could make a person do anything.

"I can't make it," I say. "Please come back."

"Jump!"

I crouch near the precipice and try to see how far down it goes. But it's bottomless. It must be. If there were an end to this, I would know.

"Tabitha," he says. "Will you come with me?"

I press my hands against my temples. Why doesn't he understand?

"I can't make it," I plead.

"What does it matter?"

What?

"Jump. Be with me."

"Please come back. Be with me here. Why are we even down here? Please…"

"Jump, Tabitha."

I can't make it. I can't do this. I can't do this! Why won't he listen? My eyes sting with a betrayal I'm trying desperately not to feel. No one has ever been so lucky. That's how it is with us, with me. He holds out his hand, as if all it would take is grabbing it.

"Everything will be fine. I promise." He watches me with those fathomless gray eyes, with that unshakeable confidence. Everything will be fine and he knows it. "I *promise*. Don't you trust me?"

I do! Absolutely! I tell him so, and I want to explain to him again, so that he'll understand, that I simply cannot do what he can do. And I wish, so much, that I could. But I can't. I can't find the words.

And he stands there, the beautiful bastard, smiling at me and holding out his hand like it's the easiest thing in the world. He holds out his hand like it's for no one but me to take. No one has ever been so lucky. That's how it's always been with us.

I whisper, "Are you real?"

"No one loves you like I do."

He's right. What else can I do?

I jump.

He laughs his easy, joyful, manic laugh.

It comes after me as the world falls away.

I hear a creak and a sharp plastic click.

Of course, I've been hearing noises all day. They're inescapable, coming from all directions as I lie in bed still.

I dreamed that I'd fallen hopelessly in love and I dove into the open void above.

How long ago was that? What's-her-name (what *was* her name?) has been lifeless and gone now for two whole days, and life goes on because it must. Rip in pieces and all, of course, of course, but, for most of us, life must go on. That's the theory, at least.

I sit up but I don't see anything. It's so dark these days. But I heard a creak and I heard a sharp plastic click, and they were coming from inside the room.

"I thought you'd be asleep."

She steps into the yellow light of the window, with her yellow-white hair and yellow-white hands, with her yellow-yellow hoodie and yellow-black ripped jeans. It's been thirteen days since I saw her face colored by anything but memory.

The face, the yellow-white one in the here and now, tilts to one side. The lips purse and the brows furrow. Emma listens to the whispering water in the pipes, the creaks in the floorboards, the sharp plastic clicks that are definitely coming from inside the room.

"How'd you get in here?"

Emma jumps, as if she'd forgotten I was here. "What?" she says, after a pause.

"How did you get in?"

"I came in through the window."

"I would've heard you."

"You were sleeping."

"I would've heard you."

"Mm."

She sits on the edge of the twin-size mattress I keep on the floor and looks around at the mostly bare room. She's only inches from my mostly bare leg. Emma says, "Your light bulb's out."

"Sure is."

After considering my answer, she asks, "How long has it been out?"

"A couple of weeks?" I hazard. "I don't remember."

"So, you just live in darkness."

"Yeah." I'm honestly not sure what she expected. She moves her hand and it brushes against my calf for a second.

"What if you need to read something?"

"I don't."

"Mm."

Emma shifts a little and settles into a cross-legged slouch. Her thigh is almost on top of my foot and she doesn't move away. I ask, "How do you know where I live?"

She hesitates before answering, "I followed you."

"When?"

"First time we met."

Imagine I'd actually gone ahead with following her that time.

Have you heard the one about the two shadows tailing and circling each other for all eternity?

Well, here they are:

"How did you get in?"

"The window, *fuck*."

"I was *awake*! I would've *heard* you."

"Maybe you dozed off."

"I didn't." Why won't she just fucking tell me?

She gives me a look, and says, "Do you believe in magic?"

"No." Yes.

"Well, I magicked my way in here."

Fine.

"Fine," I say.

She shrugs, as if some people just can't be helped. As if I'm a lost cause and she'd be better off leaving and forgetting me forever. As if she might do just that.

Please don't.

"Don't get so worked up, loser."

"What do you want?"

"Been a while," she says.

"What do you want?" I repeat, but without the edge.

"Have you been holed up in here all this time?"

Is that a hint of concern in her voice? Something tiny in my chest stirs, just a little bit, for just a little moment. I think it might be a parasite, of the little chest type, and it might sail off into the starfield if I'm not careful. I answer, "What does it matter?"

"Shut up," she says. "Sometimes things matter. Have you just been sitting here?"

"Sometimes I get up, go out. I'm looking for my— Jorge... My friend. He's missing."

"Did you call the cops?"

I didn't.

"You *are* looking for him?"

I am!

Emma doesn't say anything. I can't tell if she believes me. I'm not sure anymore if I believe me.

"I went back to that factory," I tell her. "That abandoned one where I met your friends. I didn't see anyone there."

"Why would you go *there*, dongus?"

"I—well, maybe Jorge would be there. Who knows?"

"Yeah? You thought your made-up friend was hiding in a *factory*? Well... Was he?"

Jorge's not made-up. He's my friend. He told me so, by the big trash can. And he's missing now. A piece of me wants to find a way to throw Emma's cruelty back in her face, but then what could she do with mine?

"I haven't seen you at the coffee shop at all since then," Emma says eventually. "Thought maybe you were mad about something dumb."

Fuck.

Have you heard the one about the idiot who thought he'd been abandoned when all along he'd been going to the wrong place?

"Why does it have to be something dumb?"

"Because I know you, Jason." She looks at me and smirks and raises one eyebrow for a second. I think she does it when she thinks she's been clever.

"Jace," I correct her. Apparently, she doesn't know me as well as she thinks.

She doesn't respond. This is embarrassing. I say, "I didn't think to go there."

"Mm. Well, that wasn't very clever of you, huh?"

Emma uncurls and crawls up the bed straddling me, pushing me back against the wall with her proximity alone, even though I'm confident at this point that she's not a ghost and could push me physically too.

She leans forward on her arms. I can feel her breath on my face. Her eyes stare into mine. They look faintly unfocused.

"Are you on something?"

"I don't do drugs. Do you?"

"No. But—"

"Good."

"Is some—are you alright?"

"Maybe I had a drink or two. So what?"

"Oh."

"Don't say something stupid, Jace."

"I wasn't going to."

"And there you go." She smirks and raises one eyebrow for a second.

She kisses me. There's a faint ashtray taste to either her mouth or mine and neither of us seems to mind. She presses hard, as if out of desire, and I let her.

We touch each other. At first, we play it safe, along the cheek, the arm, the back. However many first times I've had, there's that same nervousness, that excitement, as exploring hands risk another inch, and another, and another.

Her skin is a kind of soft that I'd almost forgotten. I run fingertips along a collarbone, around the base of her neck, through the thick hair falling down her back. I slip my hand into the seat of her pants and give a squeeze to what little I find. I won't be an ass man tonight, but, on the other hand, I trace a tight stomach and the tremendous rack she's been hiding in her constantly baggy clothes.

Her long fingers run through my hair, over my torso—lightly toned by default as a consequence of being an anemic slug—grab the edge of my shirt and pull it over my head.

I kiss her neck and the line of her jaw, slide a hand under her shirt and the cup of her bra, nibble at an earlobe. For a second, just a second there, she doesn't move, doesn't even breathe. She sighs. I linger.

What makes her hold me closer? What draws a moan from her? What steals her breath? I greedily take as much of her as I can. I don't know if I'll ever get another chance.

When I get to the hollow of her neck, Emma pulls back. She removes her sweater and tosses it to the floor. As she's undoing the bra hooks behind her back, she says, "You know, I usually don't sleep with Asian guys."

Bitch. "Same."

Emma sits back and laughs, apologizes for the wrong thing, laughs again. She sits there for a moment looking at me.

In the same moment, she starts moving to cover the distance between us and I start talking to cover the silence:

"You said—"

She pauses with a start, pulls back slightly.

"—I don't—"

Oh, God. Why can't I stop?

"—get the girl."

I'm a fucking moron. Why didn't you stop me?

Emma sits back and burns me with her glare.

"You are seriously *such* a fucking jackass," she says. "Listen, stupid. You're not getting the girl. Okay? Do you want to fuck or not?"

Shit. "I'm still deciding."

Emma laughs and, hopefully, forgives my comment. Or forgets about it, at least.

I pull her down onto the bed and she comes with me. I wish I were able to throw her around, without needing her to throw herself a bit to assist, but then we come back to my aforementioned anemic slug status.

She helps me tug her pants off and opens her legs as I slide my hand down her stomach. I slip a finger into her, and then give her a second, and then give her a second to relax before I start moving my hand, back and forth, faster and faster. We touch, taste, kiss, caress each other until she gets too close to focus on anything but feeling.

She buries her head into my shoulder, panting, and bites softly into my flesh when she finishes. I keep going a little longer, for good measure, until she pushes my hand away.

She can't say I'm not a good host.

We lie together for some time, as her breath comes back to her and I idly fondle her breasts. Several times, I almost say something. She places her fingers on the back of my neck.

As we start getting back into it, Emma catches me with my guard down and briefly licks at my male nipple. I don't mind it, if I'm being totally honest, but I would never be totally honest about such a thing.

Just to be safe, I whisper, "No homo."

She laughs into my chest, and then pulls back and looks at me, and then smirks and does the eyebrow thing, and then removes my pants. I have to help her with that, of course. She strokes my cock and then stops and just holds it for an impromptu penis inspection.

"Oh," she says. "You're not small."

Rude. "You expected me to be?"

"Well… You know…"

I'm used to this sort of thing by now, you understand, but, to mess with her, I tell her, "I *don't* know. What?"

"Because that stereotype about Asian guys…"

"What about Asian guys?"

"They've got little wieners."

The smirk, the eyebrow. She says, "Thought I wouldn't say it? Don't be a little wiener."

The look turns greedy and she starts stroking me again. I'm not sure if that's enough for me to let the shitty comment go.

Still playing with it, she leans in like she's going to tell me a secret, and plants a kiss somewhere that might be my neck or my back or my shoulder. She breathes her secret: "I want to feel you inside me."

I'm ready to let the shitty comment go.

Emma finds a condom in the pocket of her discarded jeans—how confident was she that this was going to happen?

She winces as I enter her. She says it hurts, but in a good way. Maybe she's just being a good guest like I'm being a good host? The prostitutes never say it hurts. Then again, they've got marathon holes.

In any case, she seems to be enjoying herself. I pause half-submerged to put her legs over my shoulders. Now she *really* seems to be enjoying herself. As far as I can tell.

Emma's a quiet lay, it turns out. I think she's a spy. Never let your enemies know you're enjoying it.

While shifting position, my foot slips and I tumble off the mattress. She giggles at my slapstick as I climb back on top of her. We find ourselves breaking out into giddy little bursts of laughter as we continue, getting absorbed back into the act only to set each other off again.

It's been a long, long time since I've laughed with someone like this.

I try to gauge how Emma might react to a hand on the throat, or perhaps butt stuff... Or even asking her to call me *papi*. I'm not sure if I'm into that, but it seems a waste to not at least try it with an alleged Latina. But maybe I ought to save the extras for later; I'm not paying for it, after all. I hope.

She suddenly smacks me lightly on the forehead, and not in a sexy way. She seems just as shocked as me by her own actions, and is on the verge of cracking up as she reminds me to get out of my head. I'm not sure I really know how, if I'm being honest, but now we can't stop laughing at the absurdity of this interaction while I'm literally inside her. We keep going, laughing together, and I try to not get smacked again.

Emma finishes before me—thanks, porn addiction. After recovering, she notices that I'm still hard, removes the condom, and wraps her lips around my cock. Refreshingly, she really gives it her full attention. I tell her she's amazing at it. She is, but I would say so even if she weren't, because I'm such a good host.

Disappointingly, Emma gives up quickly and finishes me with her hand. While rolling away, she suggests that maybe I should shower next time.

Oh. The sniff test supports her suggestion, but, in fairness, I didn't have any warning. I just agree with her so she doesn't notice that she said that there will be a next time.

I sneak out of my room naked to piss and towel myself off. When I come back, Emma's still where I left her. I half-expected her to be gone by now. Surely, we're coming up on the hour? Does she want to cuddle? Does she not?

She's still nude, half covered by a blanket, her neck craned to examine my small attic room from where she lies

"Have you heard the one about the sexy breakfast?"

"What?"

"A man—Oh. Have you heard the one about the sexy birthday breakfast?"

She looks at me expectantly.

"A man—let's say Johnny—is telling his buddies about the birthday surprise he got from his wife. He's telling them about this incredible breakfast that she made for him. Eggs, bacon, sausage, pancakes, toast, milk… Anything he wanted, and she looked so incredibly sexy cooking it.

"Naturally, his friends need to know, 'Well, what was she wearing?'

"Brimming with pride, Johnny answers, 'She was naked to the waist!'

"After a pause, one friend asks, 'From which direction?'"

Emma doesn't seem to get it. To be fair, it's a pretty bad joke. Don't you think so?

I throw myself down on the bed next to Emma. It's not an official cuddle but you can only have so much space between two people on a poverty twin mattress.

"So, you live in *this*," she says, gesturing lazily at the room with a long arm that then flops onto me and stays there.

Rude. "Sure do," I answer.

"How depressing."

I give her a tit a pinch, just because.

Emma laughs. "You hungry?"

"Constantly."

We discuss our food options at this time of night and settle on a place. Then we dawdle for a few more minutes before getting up.

I'm struck by a stupid thought, halfway through pulling on a pair of ratty jeans, inspecting a tiny drop of wetness on my underwear that bending over has squeezed out of me. What's-her-name just *died*—and Jorge's missing, and—and a lot of people. The Moms, the Paulie Babies, you know. The theoretical ghosts of so many dead, missing, lost, gone, and here I am forgetting everyone just because I got a whiff of pussy.

Should I have abstained out of respect? A celibate wake? For how long after your passing am I not allowed to enjoy life? Am I an asshole? Would the cadavers even care or is this my own bullshit?

Please. I don't know the theory. You can't punish me if I didn't know the rules. If you know what I'm supposed to do, I'd appreciate some information here.

Emma asks me what's wrong but I deflect. It's better for us to just move on, put on our pants, and enjoy our midnight snack. That's the theory, at least.

She looks at me like she does know the rules, but she doesn't say anything about it, one way or the other.

We stroll to a taco shop, not rushing because it's one of four within walking distance that are open 24 hours, for all the midnight drunks and slow-walkers and nobodies. God bless San Diego.

Emma asks about what I've been up to but I don't know how to answer. I tell her so. She calls me stupid—naturally—and then tells me about what she's been up to: drawing, painting, cooking, looking at pictures of dogs in need of rescue, living and playing old video games with her brother, the half-black, worked-up, captain-football Danny. So, basically, fuck-all.

It takes almost an hour for us to reach the all-night taco shop. Leaning over the counter inside, I stare at the wall-mounted menu for a very long time, comparing prices and estimated portion sizes as the lady at the cash register judges me with her sleepy eyes.

This is the only kind of math I can manage. Although I missed the arithmetic gene that would've made me a full-blooded Korean, there are some unavoidable calculations that come with being fucking broke. I just hope she thinks I'm indecisive instead of a God damn peasant.

"Hey," Emma says. "Do you want to share a jesus fries?"

"What's a Jesus fries?"

"Jesus fries. Carne asada fries with a fried egg on top. Jesus, how long have you lived in San Diego?"

"Uh…" Shit. I can't remember. "Two years?"

"You should get out more."

I should have more money. I shrug. "Sure," I say. "We can split."

"My treat."

"Why? We can just split it."

"Because I'm a modern woman. Shut up."

I put my hands up and gesture for her to go in front of me.

What did she mean by that? Maybe she thinks I can't afford to eat. After all, she did see my room, and my ribs. This whole situation is looking suboptimal for me, but free food is free food. Right?

"I'll get you next time," I tell her.

"Mmhm."

What does that mean?

The cashier lady doesn't know what Jesus fries are either and Emma has to order in long-form. Her expression dares me to say anything. I don't rise to the challenge, of course, since I'm not prepared to offer up the cash for my half of the meal.

We sit down at a table to wait for our food. I notice for the first time that her eyes are hazel, which I think might just be brown but for girls. And maybe she doesn't look so sickly as I'd originally thought. Maybe.

A couple of the late-night drunks are stealing glances at Emma. There's a kind of petty satisfaction in being with the girl other people are admiring. I would never say that out loud, of course. What might people think?

Emma gives me a knowing look. The smirk, the eyebrow. It's a little less attractive if she notices herself, but I would never say that out loud. She rolls her eyes in a way that's a little cute and a little annoying. Then, yawning, she puts her head down upon crossed arms.

A few strands of her long, pale hair lie on the table. Should I move it back into place? She said I haven't gotten the girl, after all, and that's a got-the-girl type of perk. But maybe I have? Will? It's so close to me, though...

"What's up?" she mumbles into her arm.

"Nothing."

Emma doesn't quite sigh but that exhalation comes close. She doesn't look up.

I gingerly take the end of a lock of hair and play with it, running my fingers along the end the way I would if I were cleaning a paintbrush. I don't know if that's the proper way to clean a brush, but that's what I would do.

She doesn't seem to notice. My heart is racing. Embarrassing.

Emma suddenly lifts her head up and says, "Jace, can you quit—"

She stops and looks down at my hands. I fold them on the table, the picture of casual. It's merely a coincidence that her hair is resting so near. She snorts and calls me a dork.

"Sorry," I say.

"No. It's fine. Keep doing it, dweeb." Is this a trap? Emma watches me tentatively reach out and take the hair. No reaction.

"What were you going to say?"

She doesn't answer. I start fanning it across my fingers again. She watches for quite a while. I wouldn't tire of this generally, but the scrutiny is killing me.

I ask again what she was going to say but she says she forgot. She says it doesn't matter. She says I should just shut up already. She says that a lot.

After some time of hair-playing and hair-playing-watching, our food is finally ready. I let go of the hair and get up to get our fries.

When I get back to the table, carrying an implausibly massive plate piled high with shit over fries, Emma and her locks are gone. Of course. Slipped out the side door. I should have seen this coming.

It was the hair thing, wasn't it? I knew that would be it. I knew she would ditch me, sooner or later.

Then she returns from around the corner with disposable forks and little plastic cups of salsa. She has to make gang signs to hold everything without spilling.

We start eating. Emma immediately stabs the egg with her fork so the yolk spills all over the fries. It's almost a game, the way we take turns to hunt and peck for the best bite. I don't know if it's quite up to the standard of a religious experience, but the fries *are* pretty good.

"What did you mean by magic?" I ask between bites.

Emma finishes chewing before saying, "What?"

"You said magic is real?"

She finishes chewing before saying, "Obviously not. I was just messing with you, stupid. Wanna go to the beach after this?"

"Okay."

I think she's lying. I think she's eating too fast. I think she's deflecting. But I have to drop it because she'll finish all the fries if I don't keep up with my fork.

As we're eating, a couple of men walk in. They must be coming from some kind of costume party, because they're dressed in such a fruity ensemble of fishnets and rainbows as to look like a homophobe had drawn his idea of what gay people are like. While in line, they're giggling and slurping and fondling each other, in a way that would be grotesque but I suppose is stunning and brave because they sandpaper each other with their cheeks.

I realize I'm staring and turn back to the food to find Emma eying me. "What's your deal?" she asks.

"What?"

"What are you staring at?"

"I'm not. Nothing."

"You got a problem with gay people?"

"What? No! I don't care. Do whatever you want, you know? I don't care. It's none of my business. I'm not like that." I'm fucking not, I swear. You know that, right?

"I'm sure. Then what?"

"Nothing."

"No, seriously. What's your deal? You look mad. Are you, like, *actually* homophobic? I have gay friends."

Imagine admitting to that.

"Let's go to the beach after this."

"Shut up. Explain."

We stare at each other for a long time. I try to scoop up another bite but Emma slaps the plastic fork out of my hand, sending it and a wad of eggy fry skittering across the floor. Rude.

"Get me another God damn fork."

She throws her fork on the floor next to it. "I'll get two, both of them blessed by god. Explain."

Wasteful. Disrespectful. Sacrilegious. Rude.

More staring.

I heave a big, stupid fucking sigh.

"Have you heard the one about the Bible thumper?"

"What?"

"So, there's this guy who's pretty into Jesus, right? One of those evangelical types. But he really dives into it when his wife and the love of his life croaks. He goes fundamental as all fuck, as you can imagine. A real Bible thumper, you know?

"He's got a couple of kids, sons, slaps them around a bit, just to keep them in line—you know how it goes. One of these kids—the baby boy of the family—he's a pretty effeminate little shit: slight build, high lisp, oriental features. You know, the works. Long, long hair, the limpest wrist you've ever seen."

"Jace."

"Of course, Bible-thumping daddy isn't crazy about how his modern little boy is turning out, but he seems to adjust to it as well as might be expected. He sits down with his son, has the ol' heart-to-heart, makes him slip into his dead mom's dress, and—"

"Oh my god."

"—Bible thumps him. Yes, God! That's the one. So, he thumps his Bible—"

"Jace."

"—in Paul's pooper."

"Jace, please."

"For four years.

"And that really thumps the faggot right out of him, let me tell you.

"And, in the wake, when it finally comes out what's been going on with that sad little homo—which one, right? *Ha*—when it finally comes out, the whole community dismisses it, sweeps it under the rug, *laughs* about it. Because '*Korean don't do like that.*'

"If anything, they insisted, it was Mom.

"Even being cancerous and dead all those years.

"And—you know what? —I get it. Sodomy is just one of those paleface things, as we all know."

No disrespect, of course. Rip in pieces and all that.

Emma looks like she's about to cry.

Why does that make me so angry?

Relentless hunger. Surrounded by rats. The fearsome hunter falls, sprawls, and lies flat. There is no sun. There is no way back.

In such circumstances, I must keep reminding myself that I'm better; this is, after all, what everything was for. I chose, and I chose right. I'm unbroken, despite the passing of my light.

I deal. I examine the hand before me. I take one card, and then another, and then whatever remains. This is the play: all-in, bluff the axons, forget the bubbling pit in my stomach, the aching fangs, and the hole in my eye.

I don't know where I am.

I stumble and I blur. I leap from locale to locale. I'm sick. I'm hurt. I think someone's following me. I draw another card. I make the wildest bets and I don't know where I am.

I glide through a shitty alley that's well beneath me. I fall into a place where rats fall. I draw.

There's someone following me, closely. She smells sterile and hungry, mostly. She smells fat, slow and clumsy. And she wants something from me. I draw.

I'm drawn. Emptied, I can barely move. I crawl, ripping open closing wounds.

It's all a mess. Now I don't know where I am. I think I'm searching the void for a heart. I just need to find the right vein. I know it's there. It has to be. It has to...

I come to an arch of ancient brick with a lone sodium lamp. There's a sickly, blurred halo in the haze. It's a crude false sun, in crude false mourning.

I can't remember the last time I saw light. I approach it warily, hungrily, like a feral animal. I'm a low thing now, a cadaverous beast, a stray. I'm lost. I'm choking and gray. I draw.

Eternal, originless, without beginning or end or beginning again. Blood drips off a fan of cards, streams down legs. The lips stitch together, punctured through over and over. The tongue swells greedily. There is nothing but pitiful eternity external. The ribs throb. The legs shake. I sit. I lie down. I'm lost. I'm...

———————————————————————

Irregular rays of daylight stab at my eyes through the shitty broken blinds.

I dreamed I only saw the sun with my mind and spirit undone.

A long, pale arm is draped loosely over me. Emma's long, pale, dumb arm. I crane my neck to look behind me and see her curled up against my back, with one foot tucked between my calves and a halo of long, pale hair spread over a wadded-up blanket she's using as a pillow.

Occasionally, I feel the hair on the back of my head move faintly in her breath. She breathes so hard for someone with so little lard holding her down.

Emma makes a small, sleepy, whiny sound and shifts closer, headbutting the base of my neck and making another small, sleepy, whiny sound. Her forehead stays pressed against my back; it makes my whole spine tingle.

I can't remember how we got here. I can't remember the last time I was held. I can't remember the last time I slept with someone—just slept. I can't remember the last time someone touched me, innocently, intentionally, without incentive.

When was the last time anyone truly valued me enough to want me around without gross payment?

I can't remember—ten or eleven or twelve, wasted away, during and after, all eleven years, a sickness in the breast or the brain, depending, I can't—I can't...

My face burns up and from the open window a sharp December chill creeps into my nose. Something wraps hot chains around my chest and throat and I choke down whatever weak garbage they're trying to squeeze out of me.

She'll stop being attracted to me if I let this happen; she'll become disgusted by the pansiness and she'll leave and she'll find someone new and forget about me forever. And maybe she'll steal from me too, even when there's nothing left to take.

I rub at my eyes with the palm of one hand. I sniffle up whatever's dripping down my lip.

What a wuss. What an egoist. What the Hell was that? It's fucking bullshit that I make *her* visitation about *me*. It's always *me* first, and *then* everyone else. Even with you, you know. Don't you think so?

Sometimes I'm not sure if you really understand what I'm talking about. Do you? Do I, even? Does she?

Probably not.

Besides, she's just here because she feels sorry for me. Because of poor Jace, with his poor, dead Mommy, with his poor, dead Paul, you dumb little queer—no offense, Paulie Baby.

If she doesn't want to be here, she doesn't have to. I don't need philanthropy fucks, for me *or* my family. We're not so broken as that. We're stronger than that. We have to tell ourselves that. I have to tell myself that. I have to get up.

I get up. I get up and I'm... tight. Something deep in my heart is stretched taut, drawing me—all the loosely associated hunks of slowly dying meat, and all the ethereal, massless me-things, and all the empty void spaces that have somehow infiltrated and become integrally me—down and in toward a core with a painful, brittle tension.

Each of the myriad puppet strings holding me together finds its end firmly grasped in my own hand. I feel I might buckle under my own weight were I not, through a marvel of not-a-real-boy engineering, pulling all the pieces rigid and propping them up.

What the fuck am I talking about?

I twitch the strings in my grip and step. Twitch again, step again. Again, and again. This isn't so bad. I think I can keep this up for the rest of my life.

I twitch over to my rickety desk and find my phone, which tells me nothing when I flip it open. When was the last time I charged it? What time is it? I look out the window. All times look more or less the same these days. I put the dumb phone back on my dumb desk.

On the way to the bathroom, applying a subtle twitch of strings, I nudge the skewed pile of papers and notebooks closer to alignment with my toe. I step into and yank up a crumpled pair of jeans. The empty, oversized coffee mug I use for soup moves from the window sill to the pile of plastic bins—I mean, dresser.

I pick up the soup mug again and study the shitty, it's-the-thought-that-counts painting of a reindeer wrapping around the outside. I consider smashing it on the floor. But, of course, that would be pretty disrespectful to Santa. Don't you think so? I put it back down on the dresser bins. Everything in its place.

I turn at the door to find Emma watching me from her coronet of ghost hair. The strings creak under the strain. Whether strings or floorboards, she heard the groaning of something, and now she's awake and alert and silently watching.

But what she's seeing happened last night, or years ago. I know what she's thinking, what you're thinking, what any sane person would think but never dare say: Why didn't I do anything? Why didn't I stop Dad?

I didn't know! What can I do if you don't tell me what's happening?

I heard, yes, but I thought they were just standard beatings, and I got mine so I thought that was fine. That was normal. I was just a little tougher about it. That's all. That's what I thought.

I didn't know.

I was just a kid.

What could I have done?

I didn't know.

Or I didn't want to know.

I don't know. Assume the worst. I deserve that much. I deserve the abandonment. Maybe that's even preferable to any kind of real accountability, the self-accusation and doubt that a guy could use to dig himself out completely.

But she has no right.

I hold her gaze, challenging her to say something.

She doesn't. I win. And what, then, do I win?

Have you heard the one about the contest to win a pickup truck?

A radio station hosted an event where contestants had to keep a hand on this truck and the last one to let go would be able to drive it home. This sort of thing happens in some parts of America.

The contest lasted for days. Many, many people fell from exhaustion, or ran off to eat, or piss, or shit, or masturbate. The body has needs, after all.

Finally, after three grueling days, the last person collapsed, leaving a young man as the winner.

The radio host, as she presented the keys to the truck, smiled her biggest, fakest smile, and said to the young man, "You *won*, sir! This brand-new truck is *yours*. I'm sure you must be *exhausted*. It's just so *amazing* what you did here these last few days. We all know the competition was *fierce*. I've never *seen* a man hold his piss for that long."

The young man, all smiles, thanked her and offered her his hand to make it official.

"No, thanks," she said, as a drop landed on her shoe.

Dumb.

I turn to sneak furtively down the stairs for a piss. Will she still be here when I get back? After doing my business, I go down to get two glasses of water, in case Emma needs more time to make her escape.

A housemate is in the kitchen. We don't speak to each other. He's tall and white and wears leather and a red mohawk, and that's really not so edgy these days but I don't feel right telling him so.

I haven't seen him in quite a while. Now that I think about it, it's been weeks since I've seen anyone living here except for What's-her-name—rip in pieces, however. Tall Mohawk could well have run off forever and I might have never known.

But here he is.

In any case, he doesn't stick around for long enough to punk me.

When I get back to my room, Emma's dressed and looking at the stuff on my little desk. She shows no shame at being caught snooping and continues flipping through a small stack of photographs.

"Rude," I say.

"Shut up."

Rude.

I hand her a glass of water. She thanks me and sips as she looks at the pictures. I go to my mattress and squat down on a corner of it, watching her.

Without pausing her review of my memories, Emma asks how old I am. I tell her and she looks a little disconcerted by my answer. She also looks much younger than twenty-five.

Can you believe that? I don't hate the idea of it, but I've never been with someone so much older than me. You might say that it's nothing compared to a fifty-three-year-old Korean man in the pooper, but it's still a little old. Don't you think so?

"It's not weird if you don't make it weird," Emma tells me. And I guess she has a point there. She holds up a picture. "Is this you?"

I can't fucking see from here. I get up to get a closer look.

Oh.

"That's Paul. Paulie Baby. As a baby."

"Oh... Paul is—" Her breath catches as she remembers.

"Dead brother, yeah. I know we all look the same to you whites—I mean Cubans—but it's easy to tell us apart. I was a much handsomer infant."

I imagine her not actually being white on a big, Cuban raft, except she's an infant and nice to me. It's such a strange image.

Emma returns the stack of photos to their place—everything in its place—and gingerly places baby Paul on top. Should be the bottom, right? Heh. That's my impression, at least. Is that offensive? No offense, of course.

She turns back to me and puts on a strained smile. "Do you want to talk abou—"

For *fuck's* sake!

She stops. She gives me a look. Did I say that out loud?

"Okay," she says. "I'll head home. I should get some work done."

"You work?"

"You don't?"

"Uh... I just got fired."

"Oh."

This is when she realizes I have no value.

"That sucks," Emma says. "I hope you get back on your feet soon."

I look down. "I'm on my feet now."

"Jackass." But she chuckles.

"What work do you do?"

"I do some freelance art." Emma looks off into space for a moment, and then continues, "And a small inheritance from my dirtnapped parents. I won't lie. Not a ton of money in commissions if you don't want to draw porn, so, well, you know."

"Can I see your art, you prude?"

"Maybe later, perv. Do you want to go to the beach tonight? Since we didn't end up going?"

Since you had a meltdown about my dumb, dead brother. You know what I mean, Paulie Baby. "Okay. Sure, I guess."

"You 'guess'. Sometimes you can be so annoying, Jace."

At least now she says my name right.

She asks for my phone number so we can make actual concrete plans, for once. I'm looking forward to finding out in advance how many weeks it'll be until we see each other again.

I tell Emma that I can't remember my number and the battery's dead. She tells me that I'm being a grumpy asshole.

We plug my phone in and sit on the edge of the bed waiting for it to charge. Emma rests her head on my shoulder, wraps her arms around my waist, leans on me until we're mostly horizontal. I show no external sign of being on the verge of tears to ensure that she'll keep holding me.

After a few minutes, Emma's able to get my number from my phone into hers, which is big and bright and tells us that it's nearly noon. I walk Emma down to the front door to see her off.

"You couldn't just magic your way back out?" I ask. I can't decide if I'm asking that to be mean.

The smirk. The eyebrow. The words: "Magic is expensive, dummy."

I don't know what to say. Why won't she show me the magic? It has to be real. Right? It has to.

"I'll see you tonight?" she says.

"Yeah. You have my number."

A long pause. I start looking around to avoid her gaze. What can she be thinking about but poor fucking Paulie Baby? Poor fucking Jace with his poor fucking Paulie Baby and his poor fucking Mommy. Just drop it!

"You okay?"

"Yeah."

"Say you're okay."

"I'm okay."

"Would you tell me if you weren't?"

"Sure."

Emma turns her head to the side and stares at me skeptically out of the corner of an eye.

What does she want from me?

Emma leans forward and slips a quick kiss through my guard, right between my cheek and the corner of my mouth. What does that mean?

Without explanation, she turns to leave.

Why do I feel so warm?

She calls something over her shoulder as she walks down the path but I don't know what it is.

I watch her disappear down the street, my breath with each step getting more ragged, more labored, more desperate.

Oh, God.

When she's gone and absolutely gone and never coming back, I go back inside, with my chest heaving, marionette strings snapping, disparate parts falling, flying, bouncing off the walls and out the windows and altogether away; and I collapse, fall, shatter, a million little pieces sliding down the grungy interior face of the front door.

It's getting cold. These pajama bottoms are worn thin, a faded plaid, whitening to senility, with a big hole in the crotch. The kitchen, with only half a light on, is just barely maintaining a border with the evening outside.

I sigh and stare into the fridge. It hums resentfully. I scan the tubs, the bags, the jugs, the bottles, the tubs again, the bags again...

What am I looking for? Something not in these tubs, bags, jugs, bottles.

The wind outside blows the dead and dying and chromatic griefs of leaves, across the lawns and skittering brisk over the kitchen window. A shiver runs through me. It's not that the heat's left my body; rather, I'm taking on cold, growing heavy and rimed, primed to sink into ice at any time.

But, then, it's about that time. It's getting to that time of year when I drive home through the retirement party of twilight and I start thinking about turning left instead of the polar and driving, driving, gone, forever and never coming back.

The fridge shrills at me. It must be aggrieved by my prolonged presence and my holy pants.

All these tubs, bags, jugs, bottles, trapped here, cold, bitter, loveless. I could make a sandwich. I could peel the clear wrap off a plate with my name on it. I could take the dog and maneuver one foot in front of the other, and then the other, and then the other, and not stop until the sun breaks.

I could drink myself to nullity, find someone to join me there, set up a permanent hideout from a whole history. The bottles are right there. And the jugs, the bags, the tubs.

There exists an unshakable feeling of want, of deprivation. There exists a hole in all existence that cries and cries to be patched up. But, in my utter deficiency, I'm unable to name a single thing I want.

In spite of all my lack, all my longing, I can't think of a single thing I desire which would slot into place and stymie the slow but never-ending release of my essence into nothing. What comes next? What would make it right?

I bet the dog would know. I bet the dog could tell me some really interesting things about what I'm missing. With such a simple life and perspective, he must know everything worth knowing. I turn to find him but stay stuck on the fridge, one hand resting on the door, the other hanging dead at my side. He's snoring faintly in the corner. Sometimes, as he dreams, he whimpers or growls softly to himself.

The mind wanders, as if lost in someone else's dream. The tubs, bags, jugs, bottles, cold, light, pants slip out of focus. They kaleidoscope together and crank the image to shards. The illusion of separation is shattered, the illusion of heat dissipated, the illusion of light smothered.

In composition, it all gains some kind of meaning I can't make sense of. But a meaning, nonetheless. Is this what I want?

I try to move toward the center but stay fixed, as if in a painting, even as it's stripped away in a desaturated blur by world-melting chemicals. I'm frozen in place. The panorama moves around me, ascending in its own chaotic, roundabout way.

A thin umbilical lifeline tethers me to a small, wretched, man-shaped thought that feels the molded plastic under finger tips, and a hand at the shoulder, increasingly—this dispersion—feathering of nosing at the knee—the guard of bone shatters and I'm exposed to something I suspect I've brought to invention—rift of—where's my line? —"Stephen!"—

It's dim when Tall Mohawk comes down from his room to go out. I'm still crumpled against the wall by the front door, but that clearly has nothing to do with him.

He looks right through me. He steps right through me. He heads out into the world. *A* world. It seems he's in one world and I'm in another. Locks? Keys?

What's-her-name would have at least seen me here if she hadn't gone and died and ghosted herself. Rip in pieces, of course.

I dreamed I froze contemplating the coming step because I couldn't see how to like what comes next.

What is the next step, though?

Well. This is as good a time as any to accept that, instead of crouching in this corner like a gremlin all day, I could have at any point pulled myself off the floor and gone back to my room. At least there I won't feel so bad about not being in anyone's way. But I stay where I am on the floor. Maybe, if I wait long enough, I'll manage to trip someone.

I check my phone to see if Emma's contacted me. She hasn't.

It feels as if something's been stolen from me. But what? What do I have left to lose? There's only so much this world can take from me before I'm not left to be taken from.

And why is it so fucking God damn dark?

I have to get out of here.

I pull myself up and out the door and out west, into the sunny, black, winter afternoon. I try to keep to the backroads and secret trespasses where I can find them, or where I can remember them from before, but I don't know Emma's hand as well as she knows the back of this city.

I wait at an intersection for the blinky little fella to usher me across, near an oblivious homeless man lounging on a bench that the few passersby conspicuously avoid.

He looks prematurely aged, battered by life, and breaded. I don't recognize his deep-fried face from the shelter but they all have that sort of look. He might be asleep, or dead, or staring listlessly at the group of teenagers doing sleepy skateboard tricks across the way.

Have you heard the one about the struggling new skateboarder?

The ramp up was tricky but the hardest part of all was the concrete on the way down.

You may remember that from back in the day. I know I do. I still wonder, from time to time, if I hit my head all those years ago trying to kick flip in Uncle Ken's basement, and everything since has been a comatose fantasy.

Imagine living in a dream world and it still being shit.

Have you heard of such a thing?

Am I still asleep and dreaming? Pinch me, please. I'll take my chances with dreams of the dirt world if *this* is the alternative.

But nobody pinches me. Nobody's listening. Nothing changes.

The light changes. The little fella blinks. The bum wakes up, looks at me and slurs out what sounds like a dazed curse. I continue on, leaving behind him and the kids and the whole drowsy scene.

Maybe they'll continue existing behind me, if this isn't all just a bad dream. I'm not hopeful.

The horizon is on fire by the time I reach La Jolla Shores. The sky darkens overhead from blood to burnt umber, to abyssal blues, back to coma nightmares that wither at my heel.

Where have I been? How did I get here? I can't remember. Would there be anything worth remembering if I were to turn around right now?

I think I left the door open.

Someone left the door to the beach open. I tie my ratty sneakers together by the laces and hang them around my neck. I don't like the way the sand shifts slightly beneath my bare feet as I walk, but that beats having it follow me home when I'm done here. I kick up little sprays of the stuff as I shuffle onto the beach. I try not to get too close to anyone.

What are all these people doing here anyway? Don't normal people have jobs right now? They're scattered across the beach in small clusters, lying around on their towels like sunning walruses. The beasts exert their bloated psychic pressure, fouling the air and water and darkening sky.

I become the lone penguin, waddling mad and unconcerned past every lounging body. I am unheeded and unheeding, unhinged and cut loose. I march unwavering into the rocky barren wilds, away from a safe coast and life.

Wenk.

Beyond the fashionable bit which moonlights as a night club, there's a long stretch of beautiful, empty beachfront. On my left, the ocean pushes and pulls, occasionally reaching far enough to grab playfully at my jeans. On my right, a steep wall rises up, separating all the rich fucks in their beach homes from losers like me.

It smells of salt and fin rot. Very quickly, the crashing waves drown out the chatter of humanity behind me. Sickly yellow lights hang above the wall at long intervals. I give their diseased glares as wide a berth as I can manage with the water penning me in.

Eventually, I come to a set of ominous-looking square buildings that loom over the shore. They have their own army of wan lights stationed along every catwalk and stairway in the shady complex.

The buildings blink and wink at me with their bloodshot eyes and I expect, if I were to climb the stairs and hop the gate, I'd find their bellies full of bunks upon bunks of troopers waiting for the order to storm the seas. I always get the feeling that I'm being watched as I pass by beneath these structures, but no one has ever stopped me and no one stops me now.

The lights end beyond the no-checkpoint, and, a bit farther on, so too does the beach. The wall closes in, choking off the beach, and then gives way to rocks and difficult terrain.

I stop when my bare foot touches gravel. I never pass this point. Something's lurking out there, waiting for the day I finally venture onto the rocks in earnest. It's nearly gotten me, more times than once. Or so I've dreamed, at least.

Here is good. I like it here. No one ever comes out this far. No thing ever comes in this far. Why would they? This is a hiding place for people addicted to hiding. And no one has ever junked as hard as I junk. And no one has ever found my stash. If they had, this shifty sand would've told me, back by the lights. The step of everything honest speaks, you know; for everything else, look for rats.

I don't know what I'm talking about.

Have you heard the one about Phaedrus and his dumb kid?

Chris once asked Phaedrus, "Dad, what should I be when I grow up?"

Phaedrus told him, "Honest."

After mulling that one over, Chris replied, "I mean, what kind of a job?"

"Any kind."

And then Chris became a hack novelist, disappointing everyone in his family and getting disowned.

I fold myself down and sit curled up with my knees to my chest and my back to the wall.

The ocean and I have a heart-to-heart. It's been some time, so it takes some time.

The ocean loves me, much in the way of the longest night, wherever I go, however far, from all the precious depths he speaks from, shaking the earth and quelling all my—

My phone starts making noises. I fish it out of my pocket and look at it. It stops ringing while I'm trying to read what it says in the little outer display. It starts again. I manage to flip it open in time.

"Jace?" Emma says.

What's she asking me for?

She sounds like a different person on the phone, but I couldn't say whom, specifically.

I can hear the gulls calling out to each other in the darkness.

"Jace?" they call out.

"Jace?" they answer.

These seagulls sound pretty stupid.

"Are you there?" she says.

What? What's wrong with her?

"Emma. What?"

"Why are you talking like that?"

I'm not talking like anything.

An ambitious wave crashes just before me in a very near miss, sending up a salty spray that reaches me in a diffuse, chilly mist. I tell her, "I'm not talking like anything."

"Oh my god. What's wrong with you? Are you fucking high?"

I don't like drugs. I like hiding. I don't like the idea of being a druggie turned something turned fucking other. Couldn't explain why, of course. You know how it is.

I shift slightly and the sand whispers to me and to the wall and to Emma, if she can hear. Do you think she can? Hear? Does she know how to listen? Do you? I do. I think I do.

Am I high? I don't think so. I couldn't afford a habit anyway. Some people are just not meant for church work.

"Have you heard the one about the nun and—"

She mutters something foreign-sounding. Then, talking normally, she says, "Shut up, Jace. I'm not waiting twenty minutes for you to stumble through some dumb joke. Are you home? Where are you? I'll come rescue you."

I hear people talking in the background on the phone. Where is she? Where am I?

"La Jolla Shores."

"Oh," she says in a little voice, even littler than the phone has made it. "You're already there. I was going to pick you up."

Pick me up? Emma has a car? Emmadora, the Cuban raft baby, ghost of come and go, has a car and can drive?

The bottoms of my jeans are slowly drying and they seem to be coming out a bit stiff.

"Jace? I need you to stay with me here."

What's she talking about? Is she with me? Is she the night or the sea? I know who's with me tonight and I know who loves me.

"I'm with you," I say, to someone.

"Stay where you are. We'll come to you."

We? Who do you think "we" is? We're already here. Right?

Emma doesn't even know where we are; this hiding place is so good.

"We?"

Emma doesn't answer. I think she hung up. Rude.

"Okay. I'll see you soon," I say, to whomever hears me.

Does anyone?

I wonder, sometimes, when caught up in my own personal silence, *Do* you hear me?

Why don't you ever answer?

The years weigh on me. I do what I can to ignore this monster of decay that rides on my shoulders.

The men who fought beside me have all faded, one by one, into first obscurity, then dementia, then oblivion. For putting our lives and spirits on the line, bringing the whole world back from the brink, rebuffing the night, slaying the dragon, turning the tide in our final hour, this is our reward and our doom. I am the last. The last. The hero who made it. Alone. Dishonored. Unremembered.

The fathoms weigh on me. I do what I can to ignore this monster of encumbrance that rides on my shoulders.

I light a candle. Small, finned-or-tentacled-or-many-legged things scurry away from my little corona. I sigh my bubbles, and command breath back into my lungs. I continue on, taking lunging steps over and around the pitted rock formations and coral.

I travel to see an old enemy. She's waiting still, I'm certain, for me to slip, for a chance to exact her revenge. But I go anyway. We'll give guarded updates on our bleak existences. We'll share our stories, bitter laughs, simmering fury. It's always been our common ground. There's nothing else left for us— through iron and fire, we shaped a world that has no place for us, for people who never wanted a place for us.

The defended, drunk on their divans, fucking my daughters, watch my straining back and assign their values to what I *must* do, as if it were a sport—a fine play here, a foul there. We burn out our souls, return scarred or not at all. And they condemn, censure, laugh, laugh. They're horrified and disgusted by what they asked us to do.

At least an enemy must look me in the eyes while trying to gouge them out. At least an enemy saw and did the same evil things. This is as close to camaraderie as exists for us now.

We don't deserve this. It doesn't seem right that we spilled our blood to build a world where our only use is spilling our blood. That wasn't the deal.

What can I do?

Maybe I should never have come back.

Maybe I need a new battle.

"Jace!" Emma calls out from nearby.

I can make her out in the darkness as she approaches, sporting yet another baggy sweater and, as far as I can tell, either stretchy, tight pants or none at all. She's walking like a dog wearing booties, lifting each foot up high and awkward with each step. Pieces of her outline stand out sharply whenever she happens to pass in front of the lights from the living part of the beach.

When she's close enough that I don't have to raise my voice, I tell her about the dream I was having. I stop. Was I sleeping? Was I dreaming? I was the vanquisher, hero of the brutal pits, but then had survived and long outlived my usefulness.

I think.

The ocean was there... But, then, the ocean is here. But, then, Emma is here.

Does that prove anything?

Emma's face, which begins with the patient expression of a first-time mother, turns confused, and then annoyed, and then says, "Good story, idiot."

"Say it in Spanish, Emmadora."

"Maricón, no me llamas asi... Buen cuento, idiota."

Why does that make me giggle?

I missed you, I almost say. But that would come off super needy. I'll just swallow that one.

I force the corners of my mouth back down. Experience has taught me that people don't like people who miss them. You know how it is.

Emma carefully lowers herself to the ground in front of me. She smiles at me, in a way that doesn't feel particularly mocking or mean. "Hey," she says gently. "What are you doing all the way out here?"

"Why are you walking funny?"

"Ladies first, stupid."

Rude. "No one ever comes here," I explain. "It's a good hiding place."

Emma stares off toward the ocean, not speaking. Probably not even listening. I barely register in her world—I've always known this. Meanwhile, I can see her so clearly when everything else is murk. She almost seems to have a faint glow of her own. I look up and there's a wedge of moon watching us, so that makes sense. I guess.

"I didn't know where to go," I add loudly, to get her attention, to make her say something. "So, I came here to wait for you."

Emma remains silent, remains distracted by waves. I don't like this. Why even come out here if you don't want me? If you don't want to be here, just fuck off.

"Relax, dummy," Emma says finally, turning her head back to me. "I don't want to get sand in my shoes."

"What?"

"Careful steps. To not get sand in my shoes."

"Oh. Should've taken them off, like I did."

"But then I have to carry my shoes all day."

"Tie them up and hang them around your neck. Dummy." Don't worry. Emma loves insults.

Emma reaches out and gropes along my shoulder with her long fingers until she finds a sneaker. Like a blind person. Can't she see by her moonlight?

"I was wondering what that was. You need new shoes," she says. Then her hand slides up to my chin and she leans forward to kiss me. Something in me glows for an instant, like a flash of stolen light.

"You couldn't see it?"

I watch as Emma carefully takes off her sneakers, stuffs her mismatched socks into them, and ties them together by the laces. That was my idea, I hope she remembers.

"It's dark," she finally answers, while reaching over to hang the shoes around my neck.

"Rude."

"What?"

"Didn't even ask."

"Oh, Jace," Emma says, in a sarcastically saccharine tone. "Won't you *please* hold my shoes, dear? Oh, *won't* you? I couldn't *possibly* with my dainty little lady bones! Please say you will! Oh, please do!"

If I ignore her constant, never-ending, garbage attitude, the words do something strange and confusing to me so I will, in fact, carry Emma's shoes. For now. I try not to grin at her. I'm not sure if she can see me not grinning, though.

"How'd you find me?" I ask.

"You told me where you were."

"But out here? This is a really good hiding place."

"What's good about it? *I* found you. You're a pretty predictable person, Jace."

Should I feel bad about that?

"You okay?"

"I'm okay."

"Say you're—oh. No fun. What are you doing out here?"

"I told you."

"Normal, okay people don't hide at the darkest corner of the beach staring out to sea."

"Did you think I was *normal?*"

"Oh my god." Emma throws her hands up—just like that night we first met—and slaps them down on her thighs. She sighs in this annoying, huffy way and says, "Fuck, Jace. Why…"

Why *what?* I was just joking. What's she so mad about?

After a moment to collect her insults, she continues, "Why do you—I mean, so some bad stuff happened to you, and that really sucks. Okay? Your family, your job, whatever. And me, I'm sure. I get it, Jason. Okay? I *get* it. I *really* do. That sort of thing *definitely* has an impact. I know it does. But *why*, Jason, why do you fight so hard to stay the person that your trauma made you?"

Oh.

It was a joke. Fuck.

I have nothing else. Changing is forgetting. But I can't tell her. I can't let her tear it apart.

It was just a joke.

And it's Jace.

"Have you heard the one about the monk and his shameful vow of silence?"

"What?"

"He didn't like to talk about it."

That annoying, huffy sigh. "That was terrible, even for *you.*"

Rude.

Emma's forehead bumps hard against my shoulder and slides unceremoniously up to the base of my neck. That annoying, huffy sigh, puffing across my throat. She probably has shoelaces digging into her cheek.

"You've got a pretty small head for your body," I inform her.

"Shut up. Let me lean for a while."

I acquiesce. Emma leans on me, gradually letting herself fall over until I've got sand in my hair and she's draped over me like a blanket. It's nice, aside from the sand and the shoes pressed into my side.

As I'm on the verge of falling into a dream, Emma climbs off me and stands up. I hold up my arms and she, not without some struggle, helps me up beside her. I still have to do most of the work. What's the point of being so tall if you can't even lift a Jace on your own?

"Come on," she says, leading me back toward life. She doesn't answer when I ask where we're going.

We stop by the no-checkpoint, beneath the last light before it becomes my world. I try to warn her about the watchers but Emma ignores me.

"I want to show you something," she says.

"I've already seen them."

She laughs, and then tells me to shut up. Something in my chest gets tight when I see the way she tilts her head and smiles at me.

"Oh!" she says, looking down and rummaging in the pockets of her big hoodie. "I wanted to show you *this.*"

Emma pulls out a plastic grocery bag tied at the mouth. She picks apart the knot and carefully pulls out a dull tan marble.

"Here," she says. She offers me the marble. I take it.

"Thanks?" I've always wanted a single marble.

"Oh my god. Stop being a shithead."

"I didn't say anything."

"Look. Shut up. Don't be stupid. Throw it."

"Why?"

"Just throw it."

I look at the marble in my palm for a moment. What's the trick? I don't want to be tricked.

I pull my arm back and throw the marble as hard as I can into the ocean.

"What the fuck—" Emma says.

"—are you doing?!" Emma calls, from far behind me.

My pants are wet. I look down. The water is halfway up my thighs and a receding wave tries weakly to sweep my legs out from under me.

What.

What.

I turn around to see Emma standing on the last patch of dry sand, visibly frustrated even from this distance. She throws up her hands when she sees me looking, as if to say, again, "What the fuck are you doing?!"

As I'm standing there, staring back at her, the sea tackles me from behind. I'm carried sputtering and flailing back to shore, with a gross piece of kelp caught on my ankle.

Emma grabs me by the arm and tries to pull me out of the surf. My waterlogged clothes fight us but we manage to get back onto land. "You're lucky you throw like a girl," she says. Rude. "Why the fuck did you throw it into the water?"

"You said throw it."

"Not into the ocean, stupid."

She didn't specify where to throw it, but who wants to argue when completely soaked? This is probably Emma's fault, somehow. I ask, "What *was* that?"

Emma pulls another drab marble out of the bag and holds it up between index finger and thumb for me to see. I find myself staring past her hand at this unconscious, deeply proud, show-and-tell smile she has on her face while she looks at her little trophy. I'm not sure if I've ever seen her smile like that, with her dumb, wide mouth.

"Hey, Jace. Wake up. Look. The trick pea, stupid."

Oh. Right.

"Trick pea? That's a stupid name. What is it?"

"You're a stupid name. It's a trick pea. I just told you, dummy."

"What's it for?"

"You throw it and go where it lands."

"Oh." What? Wait. "Like magic?"

"Obviously."

Jesus Christ. "Really? Magic-magic? Or trick-magic? Is it a trick?"

"How would a trick do that? It's magic, obviously."

"Is this a prank? Are you fucking with me?"

"Stop being dumb, Jace."

"You better not be fucking with me… *That's* what just soaked my clothes?"

"You did that to yourself."

No, I didn't.

I sit heavily onto the sand.

Magic is real. Magic is real? Magic is *real!*

I knew it! I've always known! I want to believe this so badly. Am I a wizard? Should I try to cast a spell? Does being able to use the marble mean that I have *the gift?*

Emma kneels down next to me. "You okay?"

I nod. Emma sits back on her heels and watches me for some time. "This is how I got in your room."

That makes sense. Right? She even said it was magic! "That makes sense. So, you can just go anywhere you want?"

"Well, you still have to land the throw. And they're kind of expensive."

"Oh."

"What?"

"I was going to ask if I could do another."

Emma hesitates for the briefest of moments before handing me the marble. It weighs almost nothing. I get no sense of power from it or anything. It just feels like an ordinary little ball of glass. I look up at Emma.

"How many of these do you have?"

"Six left, including that one."

"What did you pay for them?"

"I got these as a gift. Or repayment, for a favor. They're a little defective."

"*Defective?* You gave me *defective* magic?"

"Sometimes they don't work. Just fizzle when you throw them. Nothing dangerous, as far as I know."

"'As far as you know?'"

"Well… Look. Angela's super sweet, but sometimes she can get a bit, um, flexible, when it comes to her business."

"Angela made these?"

"Yep."

"*Flexible?*"

"Trust me. She wouldn't give me anything that would hurt me. The worst she'll do is… offer me some trick peas instead of money and wait for me to ask before disclosing that it was a bad batch."

"Oh. She'll just rip you off, is all. No problem."

"Don't say it like that. I've only had two duds so far. That's pretty good, in my book." Shrugging, she adds, "She's really nice. I guess it's just that her customers have higher standards than I do. How else could you explain me hanging around you?"

"What do her customers use these for?"

"Doesn't matter. She's just doing business. She's a good person."

It's strange that Emma would befriend such an unscrupulous cow. I'm not talking about myself, if that's what you're thinking. Don't be rude.

"Have you heard the one about the nicest swindler?"

"Jace. *Drop it.* She's my friend."

Fine. "What was the favor?"

"Don't worry about it. Are you going to throw it or not? Try not to drown yourself this time. If you're being an idiot, it can still hurt you *that* way."

I look at the marble in my hand. Is this wasteful? I guess she wouldn't have given me one if she really wanted to save them. Or she shouldn't have, at least. It's her own fault, really.

Have you heard the one about Emma's generosity?

Everyone knew she'd lost her marbles when she gave away all her expensive magical knickknacks.

"Are you sure it's okay to waste the marble?"

"Don't worry about it. All you have to do is open the door and I no longer really have a use for them."

I toss the trick pea underhand over Emma's head and watch it descend toward the sand.

There's no sound, no light, no smoke, no mirror. I'm just sitting behind Emma now. Neat.

She gets up and walks over. "Satisfied?"

"What stops my leg from phasing through the ground when I use it?"

"I don't know. Magic."

"How does it work?"

"I don't know."

"How do you not know?"

"Do you know how a car works?"

"Are you a witch?"

"No."

"But witches are real? Angela's one?"

"I think they don't like being called that."

"Why?"

"It's considered offensive. They used to burn you for that."

"What should I call them?"

"Angela says, 'artist'."

"So, Angela *is* a witch?"

"What did I *just* say? She's an *artist.*"

"And you're an artist too."

"Well, yeah… But not like that. I just draw and stuff."

"Oh. That's dumb."

"You're dumb," Emma snaps.

Did I offend her or does she just reflexively insult me? Both? Is she actually a witch? Maybe she pretends to be an artist to hide that she's an artist.

I ask, "Are ghosts real?"

"Uh. I don't know."

"Zombies?"

"Never heard of one."

"Is there a Heaven?"

Instead of replying, Emma just shrugs and gives me a kind-of-sad, kind-of-apologetic, Hell-if-I-know smile. What good is she if she can't answer any of my eternal questions that have never been answered?

"What are you?"

"What?"

"You're not a witch, but you're *something*, right?"

"*Artist.* And no. I just buy stuff sometimes if I need it. Or gifts, I guess."

"Oh. It feels… wrong, that magical items are bought and sold like that. Like a—like a waffle maker."

"A *waffle maker?*" she laughs. "Oh my god. Look. Do you think labor should be free just because you don't understand it?"

Maybe. The smirk, the eyebrow. She thinks she's so clever.

"Could *I* buy magic things, then? Am I a member of the secret magical underworld now? Or do I need to be initiated or sponsored or something?"

"All you have to do is find someone and have the money." Emma gives me a resigned sort of look. "It's really just the loose community of losers you've already met. That's all there is to it. Almost always outcasts, for some reason."

Oh. "I—I don't know. I guess I've always been sure that there's just this whole hidden world out there." A world where I belong.

Another shrug. "That's it," she trills. "There aren't as many people out here as you probably think. And not everyone is, you know, paranormal."

"Oh. Okay. Cool."

Emma tilts her head and looks at me like at a thing in a jar. "You know, Jace, I thought this would make your day, your month, your *whole life*. Only you could get something he's wanted all his life and still find a way to be disappointed."

Fuck you. "No! I'm not disappointed. This is just all really new to me. There's a lot to take in. Okay?"

"Mm."

"Really!"

"Sorry. I shouldn't make fun of you. Look. I'm sorry the fantasy world isn't *your* fantasy." She pauses for a moment. "Seriously. I'm not making fun of you here. If it makes you feel any better, I could be wrong. Everything I've seen is really... I don't know. Scattered? Disconnected? So, there's plenty I don't know. Could be tons of epic sorcerers out there that I've never met, just waiting to meet you. Maybe we out here are some uncontacted tribe of backward, spear-chucking jungle wizards."

"You *are* making fun of me."

"A little," Emma says, fishing for something in a strangely low pocket on her pants. "Get over it."

She pulls out her phone and lights her face with a blue glow. She reads something and then tap, tap, taps a quick response.

"Let's go find the others. Yeah?"

"Others?"

"My brother and Angela are here. I told them I'd come find you."

"Oh. Just the two of them?"

"Who else? Isabel? Your best friend, Sebastian?"

"Who?"

"Are you serious?"

"The first one."

"The cute little girl with the hot dog."

Oh. I thought maybe Emma had forgotten about that. I say, "Oh. Right... And no Sebastian?"

"He's probably somewhere getting high and feeling better than us. Why? Were you hoping to not talk to him again?"

"I was just wondering... Can I ask Angela about her defective witchcraft?"

"Well, don't call it that. And I wouldn't... I think she might—"

"Is Sebastian a werewolf?"

Emma laughs so hard that she falls over.

I think that means he is.

Angela and Danny are almost all the way back to the party part of the beach, basking in the glow of the smallest, most remote public fire pit. It looks like half of the fuel is trash.

They're sitting very close together, even though the worn towel they're sharing allows for plenty of room for at least a Jesus and a half in between. Angela absently traces arcane symbols on his forearm with her pudgy little fingers. He doesn't appear to mind, one way or another.

Curious.

I don't mean to be mean, but I feel like maybe he could do better. Then again, I shouldn't be commenting on who deserves better than whom.

She greets us enthusiastically when we arrive, and asks where we've been, and sees my waterlogged self and asks what happened. He passes us red plastic cups with small amounts of what smells like vodka, and says, "You're not dead yet?"

"Oh, Danny, no!"

"Don't be an asshole, Danny."

Maybe I was wrong. He *can't* do better. Why would he say such a thing? The asshole.

But Emma did stand up for me. My knightess in shining armor. Does she think I'm weak? Will she stop liking me if I'm weak? How do I stop being weak?

Danny doesn't apologize. He tells me to relax because it was just a joke. He offers a dismissive wave of the hand.

It's the hand that Angela's not attached to, if you're trying to picture the scene.

No one cares if he apologizes, I guess. The girls have already moved on.

Fine. Whatever. The moment passes. I take a polite sip of lukewarm vodka and lower myself to the sand.

Emma moves to the far side of the fire and plops herself down next to Angela, right on the edge of the towel. Why didn't she sit with me? Is it over? That's it? *Wham, bir*, thank you, sir?

I'm sure everyone's aware of how strange it looks that I'm here on my side and everyone else is clustered over there. But it would be stranger still if I moved, especially because you and I both know that I belong here, separate, apart, quarantined for being too weird.

Danny asks how I've been, and it doesn't sound mean this time but I still don't want to say something that will make him mock me. Do I answer normally or should I play it off with a joke? Does he actually care at all or should I just tell him that things are fantastic?

He loses interest before I figure out how to respond.

Angela asks again what happened, looking at me, but clearly expecting Emma to explain. She does, in broad terms, not mentioning the marble—the trick pea. Stupid name.

"I threw your trick pea," I add to Emma's story. "It tricked me."

Angela looks puzzled, then at Emma, who's glaring at me. I think they don't get it.

"What's a trick pea?" Angela asks.

What?

"That's what Emma calls your blink pearls," Danny says.

"Oh!"

Emma mumbles, "'Cause they look like little garbanzos."

Angela practically squeals at that. "That's *adorable*, Emma! I'm going to call them trick peas from now on. Imagine the marketing!"

Adorable Emma. Emmadora. Emmadorable. Heh.

To distract everyone from Emma's shame, I ask, "So, Angela, you're... an *artist*?"

She smiles big and wide. "Oh, yes, Jace. I am!"

Emma's sitting with her shoulders hunched and her head down, not making eye contact with anyone. It's Emmadorable.

"How'd you become that? A-an artist, I mean. I would've thought more people in this... you know, community, would be... Uh. Artistic."

Emma has her head tilted back, emptying her cup in one big gulp. It's not as Emmadorable. Danny watches me and I can't tell what his expression means.

"We-e-ll," Angela begins. "*I* learned from my mother, sweetie."

"Oh. So, it's hereditary?"

"Maybe! I don't really know, sweetie. It seems like it could be, doesn't it, *sweetie*?"

"Oh. I thought maybe you would know... How do you do it? How'd you make the trick peas?"

"Well, *sweetie*, you have to choose the right elements and mix them just right. It's an art, really."

"Like fire and water and wind and stuff?"

"More like Radiance, Void, Barrier, Origin, you know?"

I don't know. "What are those? Is that what trick—"

"Jace," Emma says. "Stop prying into her business."

"Oh. I wasn't trying—Sorry."

"Oh, it's no problem at all, sweetie."

"How do you find customers?"

"Oh, sweetie, just word-of-mouth, really. Sometimes special requests online if they find me and it's not too far."

"Do wizards secretly control the world?"

"No, *sweetie.*"

"But, if you're stronger than everyone, couldn't you just use your powers and conquer everything?"

"Well, *shit*, Jace," Emma snaps. "This isn't Baby's First Fairy Tale. Unfortunately for all the grand wizards you've got such a boner for, magic exists in the *real* world."

"That doesn't make sense."

"It makes *perfect* sense if you're not completely disconnected from reality."

"Oh, Emma, sweetie, don't be so hard on him!"

"But if you can do stuff no one else can do…"

"Nobody knows how technology works. Does being good with computers mean you can do anything you want?"

"Yes?"

"Naw," Danny says.

"No!" Emma says.

"Oh, *sweetie*, no," Angela says.

Yes?

Fine. Whatever. I sit back and stop talking.

They move on. Emma and Angela chat about… I don't know. Girl stuff. I'm not really listening, but probably boys, periods, munitions… That sort of thing. Emma's a lot nicer to her than she is to me. I think that means she likes me better.

Sometimes they look at me and lower their voices. Sometimes, when they're whispering about me, they laugh, which is not very nice. That means they like me. Right?

I want to ask Angela more about the witchcraft, but it seems like no one in the know actually *knows* anything, at least not anything they want to share with me. Besides, I don't want to come off as rude for interrupting the female bonding ritual.

Have you heard the one about the interrupting—moo!

I like that one.

Danny interrupts their conversation, like a *very* rude cow: "I've got to get going. Working early tomorrow."

Danny works? He should have mooed.

Angela and Emma protest for a minute but then rise to clean up and throw sand onto the fire. I don't see why we *all* have to leave.

"What do you do?" I ask Danny as I get up, pretending to help with the fire.

"Grease monkey."

What the Hell does that mean?

"He's a mechanic," Emma explains.

"He used to be a programmer, you know!"

"Angela, stop."

"Yeah, Angela. It's *software engineer*. Danny's *fancy*."

"Really? You were a programmer?"

"I *know*! Dumb monkey don't understand *none* of the Chinese magic box com-pew-turrs, right?"

"No, I meant—"

"Wow, Jace. Just say you hate the negroes already."

"Emma! *Please* don't use that *word*!"

"That's what you were thinking, right?"

"No—she said—no…"

"Come on. Say it. Bitch. Say it."

He shows his teeth. Emma's bent double laughing.

Fuck. I'm not racist. *She's* the one who said it! I need to get out of here.

"No, I didn't mean…"

I need to get out of here.

"Oh, Danny, stop it. Emma! Be nice!"

Emma calms down enough to say, "Alright, Danny, stop. Stop picking on the slow kid."

"I was just fucking with you, son. Don't cry." He's still leering at me in that weird, bullying way that enrages me, all the more so because it also scares me. He puts a hand on my shoulder and I hate it.

"Asshole. Let's go, guys. Mr. *Software Engineer* has to grease the monkeys in the morning."

I need to get out of here.

Danny and Angela start walking back toward the parking lot but I don't follow. I don't want to be in the car with him.

If I stay here and they go, it's like I've gotten out of here.

Emma stays where she is, watching me stay where I am. I'm sure she'll join them any second now. I always knew she would leave me.

She throws her hands up. She walks to me, calling something over her shoulder to the others, who continue on as if they can't wait to get away from me.

"Jace? You coming?"

I remove her soggy shoes from around my neck and hold them out to her. "I'll just walk home."

"Oh my god. Don't be a baby. She's not even that mad at you. Come on."

"What?"

"Angela doesn't hold grudges. You'll be fine."

What the Hell is she talking about?

"Oh..." She looks thoughtful. "You're upset about *Danny?*"

What else could she have thought?

"I'm just going to walk," I tell her.

"Jace. Listen. Danny's a good guy. He's just an asshole sometimes. You'll get used to it."

"*He's* a good guy? Really? You think so?"

Emma pauses for a moment, huffs. She says, "Look. Don't tell him I said this—he likes to keep up this tough guy persona—but Danny's super sweet underneath that vicious sense of humor. He gave up a *really* good programmer job to move back home when I was... just fucking everything up, and I really needed someone to help me get my shit together. Danny saved my life. Really. He's a dick sometimes but it's been just us for a long time and we've always been there for each other. Okay?"

This doesn't make sense. I ask, "Why a mechanic, though?"

"He likes cars, it's close to home. It works."

"But couldn't he just do a computer job here?"

"I think he was tired of it anyway. But he probably would've stuck with it if not for me... Look. It's got nothing to do with you. Okay?"

Fucking everything up how? What does that mean? Was it drugs like her mom? I ask, "Fucking everything up how?"

"Don't worry about it. Danny cared enough to come back for me. That's the takeaway here. And he probably said something really shitty when he did. And that's okay."

"Must be nice having someone care about you."

Emma lowers her head slightly and looks at me with wide eyes. She looks like she might hit me. "Are you serious?"

I don't know what to say. I'm only serious if it doesn't get me hit.

"I'm right *here*," she says. "Do you think I'm having this stupid conversation right now because it's *fun*? Are you *serious*?"

Fuck. I'm fucking everything up. "Sorry," I say. "I didn't mean it like that. Sorry."

Does she really mean it, though? No one ever does, not really. Don't you think so?

Emma stares at me. Then she sighs and pulls me into a long hug. Her dangling shoes kick lightly at my back, but that's not the part that hurts.

She says she'll call me later. She doesn't specify when. Just later. The shoes swing as she strides away over the sand.

Look how eager she is to drop me. She left me all alone, just like that.

I always knew she would.

The waves are pitch-black and frigid and they jounce me, little by little, nearer to the shore. My instincts push to hold position but my body doesn't respond.

The legs kick. The arms paddle. But they're not doing it on *my* account.

The water is streaked with the distorted reflections of beach-party lights. The din of seawater and seabirds is occasionally broken by distant shouting and laughter.

I'm wrapped tight and absorbed into a seed of self. I huddle against a shadowed wall, trying to be invisible, but I still find me without any trouble.

I'm dark, bald, pudgy, tall, faceless, unkempt, unbelonging, graceless. I slide slowly out of my seat, pouring onto the floor like a bitter drink spilled. I stay there.

I can't sleep. I wake up sobbing on the brink of late night and early morning. Caught in a looping rip tide of confusion and misery, I'll do anything to lose me. Anything to lose me. Like everyone else.

The salt water bites continuously at my burned-out throat, sending waves of fiery agony through me. I writhe, clutch, ball up, flee. But the body doesn't respond.

I am motionless, concealed, melting into a puddle of backdrop, of no interest to anyone, but I can't make myself look away. Where else is there to look? I contain nothing I or anyone else could possibly wish to see.

I smolder. I hang. Without breath, the body sends lightning bolts of panic, up and down, up and down the spine. I gasp for gasps of air but the body doesn't respond.

I'm grasping the hand of another shell. It's a home, a community. If nothing else, it's a way out. I agree, thinking that I could abandon me for good, once and for all, wholly and finally. I could at least contribute to something greater. They take me in, extravagantly, take me out to sea. Of course, I agree.

As a sad but not ineffective consolation, I see in retrospect that consent was never a necessary piece of the formula. She could have taken me regardless.

Shriveled like a molted skin, I sit motionless on the beach for several minutes, approaching an hour, approaching an eternity in the timepiece of torment.

A thought—undermining language, undermining the dear illusions critical to being man—whatever that means. Her command wyrms its way into my skull and reverberates, violent, teeth-rattling, from temple to temple.

The body responds. It goes inert. It drifts and sinks and screams from every nerve-ending as the flashing surface fades. I vanish from view, at last.

I stare at sickly eyes in the mirror for a long time before smashing it. I claw for an escape. I accept the first kindly offer, without consideration. I'm burned, for no reason at all. I claw, claw for an escape.

The body doesn't respond.

The grating trill of digitized elevator-style music, with its melodic *beeps* and *boops* and *bliddles*. It's muffled and vibrating against my chest. My hand hurts from holding the phone so hard.

Have you heard the one about the nonfunctional concert ticket?

Ricky went to a concert for his favorite Norwegian Death Metal band and found that the ticketing system was down when he arrived. Along with a whole bunch of other would-be attendees, he was stranded out in the cold.

He noticed that there was a support hotline number printed on his ticket, so he gave it a call. They put him on hold for several minutes, and he was getting increasingly anxious as he could hear the show starting inside. Finally, he got on the line with a live customer support agent.

"Hi," Ricky said. "I'm trying to get into this concert but the thing won't read my ticket. It's already starting. Please, can you help me get this resolved?"

Giving no indication that she'd heard him at all, the agent said, "We're experiencing unusually high call volume. Please talk a little quieter."

Emma calls again.

I dreamed I surrendered myself to the fire and slipped back to witness myself on the pyre. I flip the phone open and tell her.

"I dreamed I surrendered myself—"

"What?"

"—to the fire and slipped back to wi—"

"Jace."

"—tness myself on the—"

"Jace! Shut up."

Rude. But I shut up. I wait.

"Come outside."

"What?"

"I'm outside. And I want fries. I *know* you haven't eaten today because you can't be trusted to take care of yourself like an *adult*. Let's go."

I feel like I'm being watched.

"Jace?"

"Outside what?"

"Your house? Are you being stupid on purpose?"

I've been noticed, finally. Something's noticed that I'm not the noise. There's so much of it.

"I'm not home, though."

"*What?* Where are you?"

Something's out here with me. I'm not out on the rocks. I'm not out in the water.

"Sinking?"

"What?"

"Uh…"

"Oh my god. Jace. What is it with you and phones? Stay with me here. What is your physical location at this very moment?"

I don't know. It's pulling away from me. It's pulling. I try to anchor myself to a shadow.

"I think—I think I'm at the beach."

"Oh my god. You said you were going to walk home."

"I'm here."

There's some more of that foreign muttering. Emma says, "You can be so annoying sometimes… Fine. I'll come rescue you. *Again.* I'll see you soon, dummy."

She said she's coming for me. She sounds tired.

"Thank you," I say after the line dies.

I mean it. You believe me, right?

I can save her.

She totters on the brink of my disaster, but I can push her back.

I can save her.

I fall back, away from her.

The cold at my back isn't that of beached steel and December nights.

I take the knife. I take the rope. I'm scared.

I take a deep breath.

I'm scared.

I take a deep breath.

She looks up slowly.

I take a deep breath.

Her eyes go wide.

I take a deep breath.

She starts to shout something.

Emma?

"What?"

"Emma?"

"What the fuck?"

"What?"

"How did you know I was here?"

"I—what?"

Over me topples and sprawls the weight of someone just a little too frail, just a little too breakable to be the rock I've taken her to be. She wriggles like an overgrown puppy to find the comfiest nooks to rest in, in the process elbowing my head.

"Ow."

"Sorry."

"How'd you find me?"

"Sometimes you're really predictable, Jason... How'd you know I was here? I was gonna sneak up on you."

"Sometimes you're really predictable, Emmadora."

"Jackass," she whispers just behind my ear.

"I dreamed I was nowhere. And I think you were there."

"Was that as flattering out loud as it was in your head?"

"I wasn't trying to flatter you."

"You should try it sometime," she says. "Does it ever occur to you how much of a jackass you are? How annoying? How hard it is just to be here? Maybe you should try saying something nice to me every once in a while."

What?

After some time, Emma asks, "You okay?"

I don't know. "Yeah."

"Say you're okay."

"I'm okay."

"Would you tell me if you weren't?"

"No."

"Good. Let's go eat."

Emma pecks at my cheek before using me as a support to stand up. She tries to pull me up but I still have to do most of the work myself. These lazy broads need to hit the gym.

"Ready?" she asks, and then starts marching me along without waiting for an answer. She wraps herself tight around my arm as we walk. I'm not sure what to do. She's too tall for this.

"Bend your arm so this doesn't look stupid. Dummy."

Rude. But I do it. I guess this works. I like it. We do it all the way to the parking lot.

"In-N-Out okay?" Emma asks as she points out which car I should make for the starboard side of.

It's okay.

Emma's car is red. Red makes fast cars. She drives fast, with all the windows down, and misses the turn to In-N-Out. And then the next one. How much vodka did she have before?

I look to see if she's texting or eating a breakfast burrito or something. I'm met with a vision of attentive driving I've never seen around here. Utterly focused, serious eyes glued to the road, ignoring the whipping wreath of platinum mane, both hands on the wheel, at 10 and 2 with such faithfulness that I bet she wishes she had a third hand just to cover her 6.

"I like the one in Poway," she says before I can ask where she's going.

"That's fucking *far*."

She gives a hint of a shrug. "You got anything better to do?"

I don't. She knows this. We don't address it.

The temperature plummets as we speed along Miramar, then Pomerado, then who knows where. Faint shivers start rolling out of my hollow gut. I kind of like it. The display reads, in soft white, a polar 33°F (12°C, probably, I guess. Who cares?). I didn't know that could even happen here.

Have you heard the one about the Antarctic math pirates?

They love polar coordinates because the Jacobian is $r\,dr\,d\theta$.

A high school math teacher told me that one. She tried to explain why that's funny but I still don't really get it. I failed that class.

Emma parks us way too far away, on the opposite end of the plaza. We cross the lot slowly, approaching the fluorescent witching hour burger beacon. She interlocks her cute long alien fingers with mine. I use both hands to try to pull the ice out of hers. It's kind of nice.

"I'll get this one. I owe you," I say, so she won't think I'm the destitute mooch that I am.

"Sure. Just get me animal fries, please. Well done." She hesitates, and then adds, "Can we sit outside?"

That's fine with me. The cold doesn't bother me. You simply have to not mind.

I go in and order: a #1 combo for me, grilled onions please, and animal fries for her, well-done, with the onions, I guess, she didn't say, plus a drink probably. It takes an embarrassing number of coins to pull together the total amount, and the cashier rounds me up out of pity.

Through a complex dance of pointing and miming through the glass, we determine that Emma has awful taste and likes warm root beer. She's texting someone when I bring out her disgusting drink but puts the phone away when she sees me coming. Both of us stare out into the piss-colored night. She puts her head down. I think about reaching for her cold hand but don't.

They bring our food to us outside when it's ready and steaming. I suppose it's not much trouble when the place is otherwise empty, but it's still awfully nice of them.

We eat quickly, not really talking, and then loiter for some time, drinking our drinks and shooting whatever irrelevant shit comes to mind. Emma seems to be anxious about something but I pretend not to notice; I'm enjoying myself and she can call me stupid in her own time.

A car passes with music turned up too loud. Rude.

A small, four-legged animal trots from one shadow to another, too far away to make out what it is. Maybe a coyote? I point it out but Emma doesn't seem interested.

"So, Jace. Um. Can I ask you something?"

"Only if you ask first."

"You're—" She stops, thinks for a second, laughs. She says a really mean thing in an affectionate sort of way. "Anyway. You're out of work, right?"

Damn it. "Yeah… Yeah. I need to find something new."

"You been looking?"

Damn it! I don't answer or meet her eyes.

"Okay. So, you've got some time on your hands?"

"I guess so…"

"Okay. Well. I wanted to ask you to help me with something."

She looks at me expectantly.

"Uh. Only if you ask first?" Does that work again? Not seeing much of a response this time, I continue, "What do you need?"

"I need to go on a trip. It would be cool if you came with me. To, um, Kansas."

"Way the Hell out in Kansas? *Why?* What's in Kansas?"

"Uh… Look. Jace… Um." She spends an impressive amount of time hemming and hawing, in at least two languages. I've never seen her so lost for insults.

"Sound it out," I encourage her.

"Shut up.

"Look.

"There's this, um, emergency. Like, a magic emergency. Fate of the world, sort of thing…"

"Can't be that big of an emergency if you're going to the beach and eating fries."

"Shut up. We just found out. The others are already on the way. I wanted to get you first and—I don't know… I was scared to ask, okay? I'm human and sometimes it's hard to ask for a big favor like this. Sue me."

"I just might. What good would *we* be for a magical emergency?"

"Emotional support? And, uh, Angela seems to think there's something… *interesting* about you. Maybe you have some powers, after all. Maybe not. I don't know. I couldn't say. But it's worth a shot, right?"

"I guess." I have powers?

"You got anything better to do?"

She's right. "Well, when you put it that way…"

She grins her big toothy grin. I wonder if she knows what that does to me.

She smirks, and does the thing with the eyebrow. I think she does know.

"What's the emergency, though?" I ask.

"Dark wizard activity. Duh. What else could it be?"

"And you want *me* to stop him?"

"Could be a her, you sexist. And maybe we'll find out you're the *chosen one*. Probably not, but who knows? Just come with me, dummy. It'll be fun."

"Fine, fine. Okay. Maybe we can look for Jorge on the way."

"Who?"

"Jorge?"

"I don't know who that is, Jace... Sometimes it seems like you forget you're not the only person in the universe."

But what if I am? Is there anyone else? Are you out there somewhere? Fuck.

I could have sworn I told her...

"Is Angela going?"

"Yeah, of course. She already left. Danny too."

"Is *he* magic?"

She laughs. "Obviously not. Are you serious? They're just, you know, an item."

What kind of item? I'm scared to ask her if we're an item. Instead, I ask, "And Sebastian?"

"Oh my god. This isn't a party."

"I'm just trying to understand what's going on."

"Stop trying to act smart. It's not your thing. You won't have to do anything crazy. I promise. It'll be fun."

But it's not a party. Emma looks annoyed with me so I don't say that out loud.

"Have you heard the one about the poor traveler?"

"Oh my god." She presses on her forehead with one hand, but I persevere.

"This guy, in Chicago, went up to the ticketing counter at O'Hare and asked the agent on duty how much it would cost to get him to New York.

"'That would be $600, sir,' the agent replied.

"'What?!' he shouted. 'Ridiculous! The lady at the next desk got a ticket to San Diego for only $200 and I have to pay triple that to go somewhere closer?!'

"Without missing a beat, the agent replied, 'Well, sir, her ticket is discounted because she has a layover in New York.'"

Emma doesn't laugh. After an uncomfortable silence, she asks, "What?"

"It was a joke."

"The funniest part is that you try to do the voices."

"Oh... I—I can't afford a plane ticket."

Now she laughs. "Neither can I. We're driving. We have enough time for that, at least. But we have to leave soon. Today. Or in the morning, I guess. It's late."

"Oh." Gas still costs money. I don't think I understand what's happening. I'm still going, though. I don't have anything better to do.

We return to my place and step easily through the space where I'd piled myself not too long ago. I push Emma in front of me so I can grope her as we sneak up the stairs to my room.

She, as it turns out, hates anything to do with buttholes, hers or mine or presumably anyone's. But choking is okay, not too hard, and maybe a few healthy spanks, but only a few.

We fuck sans condom, as neither of us came prepared. Don't worry. I pull out like a champ.

She wipes herself off with my shirt. Rude. When I return from cleaning myself off, she pulls me down to the bed so she can use me as a pillow.

I lie awake for a long time, listening to her breathe that loud breath.

I don't know what's happening but tomorrow she's leaving and she says I'm leaving with her and I don't know what's happening.

Also, I'm not used to going to bed so many hours before sunrise.

A cold, cold wind blows, laying fingers of frost across ribs and neurons. They quiver and ache. They rattle together with a smothered violence, shivering off tinkling spears of ice that chime like glass bells as they splinter.

I don't know anymore why I came here.

I don't know what I thought I'd find.

What I have found: The sky, celestial blue, dotted with windswept clouds, quaking with gust after heaven-wide gust. The sea, liquid desert stretching from horizon to horizon and reflecting a midnight from another time or place or thought, full of unfamiliar constellations and all the lightless expanses between them. There is no sun.

I pull tighter my coat—a patched tweed affair, utterly inappropriate for the journey—and peer over the side of the dinghy. A stranger behind dark glass stares back at me, with a look of, if anything, worried curiosity. I feel my face to trace the lines of the expression; the stranger does the same. Is this me? Is this who I am?

A sudden burst of wind buffets me, shoving me back into the bottom of the boat, whipping the loose pieces of my coat and throwing a flurry of paper overboard—

My work!

I snatch for what I can get, even as the words are steeped, drowned, and dispersed into a starry night. The stranger reaches for all the same pages. Sometimes she beats me to them.

I come back with terribly little opus in hand. I feel the meaning vanishing, baroque curlicues of abstraction leaking out into nihilism, becoming scattered patterns of sea ink and just dumb, fucking dumb chemistry.

Leaning over the edge, I eye the soaked sheets as they drift farther away, well out of range, well out of mind. Pale autumn leaves, scribbled and fallen and dead.

I look down, into the eyes of the stranger leaning out to meet me. I look past her, into the deepest, deepest, darkest waters.

Bringing myself close to the black surface, I find still no bottom. I look up and, all around, find still no shore. So far out, and for what? The thesis is pulp now. It takes on water and slips under the waves. It winks out, page by page, along winding alleys of cortex, settling to the sleep of gambles gone bust.

I sit back heavily into the boat, holding what I have left in both hands, waterlogged and ruined, blurred, now void of resolution, meaningless. I want to cry. I want to sob, ugly and undignified, and sink into the ocean to never be seen again.

My oars are gone, either carried or scuttled, away and away. My work—my life's work—my life—is gone, melted, lost to the sea, and with so much gone in the assemblage, all now wreckage, now flotsam or jetsam.

I never meant to come here, so far out, beyond the edges of any map I could find. It cost me all I had and more, now all for nothing. Absolutely nothing. Worse than nothing, a price paid, inadvertently, to trap myself in a void. All I see are horizons. There's no going back. There without a back again. There without a goal. There without anything.

I lie sprawled across the boat's floor, solitary, silent, staring wild-eyed up into the wild-eyed blue. The clouds move quickly in the fierce air streams, but never in groups, never coming together. Ships in the night, the lot of them. A sad, little boat in the night.

I crawl to the edge and hang heavily over the sea, perilously, threatening to capsize the whole capsized venture. The stranger meets me. There's a blankness in her eyes, like glass polished raw. I extend a hand to touch the mirror between us, and she reaches out for me.

I'm shaken awake by Emma, leaning over me with her wet hair hanging down into my face. She smiles down at me wordlessly.

Why is she awake now? The sun isn't even up yet. Who the Hell does that?

"Have you heard the one about the rooster and the crow?"

"What?"

"I sure fucking didn't. What time is it?"

"Normal people are up by now."

"Come on," she says, grabbing a damp lock of hair and waggling it over my nose. It smells nice. "I want to get going soon."

I sit up. Emma squats back on her heels. She's mostly dressed, in different clothes than what she had on last night.

"I dreamed I went to sea chasing a theory and found myself lost there, stranded and weary."

"What?"

"I dreamed—"

"Did that rhyme?"

"What?"

"Never mind. You're so fucking weird."

"Did you shower?"

"Obviously."

"In someone else's house, without even asking. Rude."

"And I used your roommate's body wash without asking too. Let's get going before she notices."

She comes forward to wrap her arms around me, which is cute, but then she starts trying to pull me up into a standing position. It's still a little cute. I flop deadweight into her arms to see if she can manage it without my help. She can't. We fall forward into the bed.

We stay tangled up like that for a minute or two. I start telling her about my dream but she tells me to shut up, extricates herself, and rises to go put her shoes on.

Have you heard about how white people wear their shoes inside?

I don't know why. Mom never did.

"Jace. Let's go. Get up. Get dressed. Pack some clothes for the road. I got coffee."

A tall, paper to-go cup steams on my ratty mousepad.

She doesn't even know how I like it: I don't.

Emma grabs a plain black tee from one of the piles near her and tosses it at me. I count a petulant ten seconds in my head before I do what she says. In that time, she zips up her duffel bag, which I don't remember her having last night, and stands up to face me with arms akimbo. She looks on the verge of saying something when the count's up but instead just follows me as I dig around in my tiny closet for a backpack.

She helps me pick out clothes to pack, filtering out anything torn, stained, or, in Emma's estimation, ugly. She folds the winners into fancy thirds before handing them to me to roll up and stuff into the bag. The pile of rejects is embarrassingly large at her feet by the time we run out of packing space, and it even includes the shirt with the buttons.

"Do you have enough of each thing?"

I stare at her.

"Like, enough underwear, enough socks. That sort of thing."

I stare at her.

"You didn't count."

"*You* didn't count."

We stare at each other.

Finally, Emma says, "Fine. Fuck it. Be stupid. Let's go."

She scoops up her duffle bag and strides out of the room, creaking and groaning down the stairs. I scurry behind her. When I catch up, as we approach the front door, I'm overwhelmed by a vague sense of uncertainty, but I can't think of anything to ask for which an answer would be of any help.

I settle on a pointless question, because they're all pointless. "So, you know where we're going?"

"Kansas, dingus."

"I mean, how we'll get there?"

Emma shrugs without looking back. "East. Into the sun, basically. Roads have signs. Don't worry so much."

But the world's ending. Or *a* world. Right? Emma doesn't seem all that concerned.

We toss our bags into the backseat of the red car. Should I open her door for her? No, that's dumb. Right?

Emma opens her own door and gets in. As I climb in through the passenger side, she grabs a large brown leather purse from under my butt and tosses it into the back. I've never actually seen her carrying a purse, and I've never noticed this until just now.

"You have a purse?"

With a sort of deliberate nonchalance, as she pins the key into the ignition, twists the engine to life, Emma says, "Sorry, Jace. I'm a girl. I wear makeup and smell pretty. Gonna have to keep looking for your little-penis tranny dream-girl."

I didn't mean it like that.

A bar, shivering on the shores of a gin river, a haunt of spirits quelled. Oh, well. It's full of noise makers, lost night things, and the dour owls that hound them. Strangers stumble in and out at a negligent cadence, dazed, slurring, laughing, laughing. Not at their desks, late for dinner, phones ring and ring, but of course nobody's missing. All are still accounted for, one way or another, one drink after another.

I take big, drowning gulps of a neat whiskey designed for baby sipping. A burning waste, I know. A travesty of experience, Daddy would say, I'm sure, and so on, and so on. I know! Tell it to the men who keep paying for it. I smile at them an absent, wobbly smile. They go on and on and on in their thick, watery, bubbling accents, about anything as long as it's of no consequence.

They're tall, or swarthy, or lean in a worked-for way, the kind of clean-shaven, handsome men who think they own the whole river. This isn't how I remember Him looking, but I've been out looking so long and this isn't my first time or my third or—or—and, would you look at that, my glass is near empty, and immediately another slides into my hand, and immediately a hand slides up my bare thigh, and immediately a rogue pinky slithers past my skirt hem, and immediately the current takes us away.

I laugh. We laugh, intoxicated and woozy. I spread my legs and search the room for a Face. I race the glass to the bottom. Someone jams a finger in me and orders another to chase. I'm blanking out, phase by phase, bottom to top, losing my footing as it crawls up past my waist.

What would Daddy say? They gurgle, "Let's go back to my place."

Off the edge of a padded stool, I fall laughing to my ass. I reach for the strand, or any one of the tipsy ghosts dancing after my hand. They drag me back up to the surface, laughing and stuttering a dream, and they carry me atop the flood splashing and sputtering downstream.

They know I'm not a swimmer, right? I'm just swimming for Him.

They say, "The water is fine," as they pour me my wine. The chill of night's tide tip-toes needles up my spine.

I slip, fall, dip into the stream. Helpless, I sink.

I call out for Daddy; they keep bringing me drinks.

I wake up suddenly with my cheek stinging. I look over to Emma at the wheel. She glances at me quickly before returning to the road. After a beat, she announces, high and innocent, "You're awake."

"Did you hit me?"

"Of course not."

I keep looking to see if she'll crack.

"Besides," she continues, "if I did, you deserved it, for falling asleep the second we started driving instead of keeping me company. That's just plain bad manners, okay? But, of course, I didn't and I would *never* do something like that."

She looks at me quickly. The smirk. The eyebrow.

"I didn't sleep well."

"Well, you *did* get smacked in the face."

Heh. Bitch.

Muted, poppy music slithers out of the car's speakers. Where are we? I look out my window. Everything outside is the kind of featureless desert scrub you can find anywhere within five hundred miles of where I live. So *that's* where we are.

"Where are we?"

"Five North."

I crane my neck to look out the driver-side window and see the ocean. Oh.

"Why? I thought we were going to Kentucky."

"Kansas."

"Kansas."

"Michigan."

"Michigan?"

"Kansas, dummy."

What?

She laughs at me and says, "We are. Going to Kansas."

"North Kansas?"

"Look. I just have to make a few stops along the way. Okay? *You* can drive if you think your way is better."

"But what about the world?"

"The world can wait."

"Can it? What the fuck is happening that we have to go to Kansas so urgently, but not *too* urgently that we can't stop for ice cream?"

"Jace. Look," with a frustrated edge to her voice. "I just know what I've been told. Okay? I basically know as much as you, okay?"

"And that's enough for you to drop everything and go on this big trip?"

"It was for you."

I don't have to look. I can hear the smirk, the eyebrow.

"I just—I—" I don't know what I'm trying to say.

Emma rants to herself in muted Spanish as she dramatically pulls off the highway and rattles and bumps the car onto the shoulder. "Do you want to go back? We can get you on a bus back to your crappy old life," she says. "And that'll be that."

"No!" I say, a little too fast. She didn't have to say it like that. "No. I'm just—curious, is all. Trying to understand what's happening."

Emma puts the car into park and rotates in her seat to face me, legs curled up and tangled in the seatbelt. I look out at the barren landscape, which rises into tall hills not too far out. The car shudders whenever anyone passes us at whatever reckless speed people consider normal out here.

"So, you don't actually know what's happening?"

"Dark wiz biz, is what I've been told."

"That's all you know?"

"We-ell," she begins. "I know they're Nazis. But, like, magic. Nazi warlocks, I guess, or something."

"Nazis?"

"Yeah, stupid. Nazis. Heard of them?"

"So, it's bunch of Poland-invading, master-race, gas-the-kikes Nazis? In Virginia? With magic powers?"

"Wow... They're probably the skinhead kind. Neo-Nazi rednecks... In *Kansas*. Are you doing that on purpose? It's not funny."

"Oh. I guess that makes sense." Does it? I add, "You know, I'm getting tired of the bad guy always being a Nazi."

"I too dream of the day the Nazis can just be cool guys handing out cake and rainbows. But, for now, in the real world, we'll have to stop them from killing everyone. Okay?"

"Have you heard the one about the Reformed Orthodox rabbi and Hitler?"

"Jace. Stop."

Fine. It would've been good, though.

"Fine. Do you know if they're kidnapping people? Around here?" Jorge's missing.

"I don't know. Why would you think that? Probably not, if we have to go *there*."

"This all sounds confusing, and dangerous. Are you sure about this?"

"I trust my sources."

"I mean, the decision to go at all. But, also, who's your source?"

Emma hesitates before answering. "Sebastian. Well, Angela. But she got it from him. And yes. It's the right thing to do. Right?"

"Sebastian? What would a werewolf know about the Germans?"

"Oh my god. He's not a *werewolf*."

"He's *something*!"

"...Vampire," Emma admits finally.

"Really?"

"Yep."

"*Really?*"

"Yes!"

"*Look at him!*"

Emma laughs. "I know," she says. "That's why I thought it was so funny when you called him a wolf. He probably gets that a lot, big bison of a man like that."

Well, of course, now it all makes sense. Sebastian *the Vampire*, I entirely trust as a source about world-threatening Nazi dark wizard news. Vampires just know that kind of thing. They're always keeping on top of who's doing what, those vampires. I assume.

"Does he eat people?"

"I don't know. I don't *think* so. I've heard that they get volunteer donations or something like that. But I'm scared to ask."

"Huh."

"Yep."

"Why not just eat people?"

"Same reason the three borderline homeless wizards in existence don't rule the world."

"There are only *three?*"

"I'm joking, stupid. I don't know how many. A small number, I'm pretty sure."

"Oh… I wouldn't have thought that a vampire would be friends with humans."

"I think usually they do keep to themselves. I think Sebastian's just a—I don't know. I guess he's different."

"Is he just the loser vampire who has to hang with us meat bags?"

"I guess so," she laughs.

"So, he's already on the way?"

"They left last night."

"Must be *really* serious, if the Vampire Council of Elders thinks it's worth sending in all these losers from so far away."

"Stop making shit up; it's annoying. But, yeah, I guess it's pretty serious." She pauses, looks away for a moment, and then adds, "But also remember that, you and me, we're probably not going to be useful for *anything* here. We're not going to be the heroes. We're going because—just because they put out a call for *anyone* who could get out there. And we can get out there. And maybe it'll be interesting. And, if not, we can hang with Angela. But probably we'll just do nothing while the big guys deal with it. Big guys like Sebastian, and, uh, his vampire friends."

"So, for no reason at all."

"Emotional support for our friends. Shut up."

"Does this happen a lot?"

"No idea—no—I don't know. If shit's been going down, nobody's told *me*."

"So, you've never done this before?"

"Correct." Emma shrugs. "If we can help people, we should. Right? Maybe we can find a way to be useful for a good cause, you know?"

I don't know.

"Satisfied?" she asks.

"I guess. It just seems like a big undertaking—this whole trip, all the way to Ohio, and—"

"Kansas."

"—Kansas, and it could be dangerous, and we're not even going to be useful, and you don't even know what we're walking into."

She rolls her eyes and starts shifting back into a driving position. "You'd be a lot happier with your life if you stopped expecting every*thing* and every*one* to rearrange to be perfect for *you*."

"I didn't mean it like that."

"Mm." Emma turns away to confer with the road. I guess we're done, then. She waits for an opening and then pulls back onto the highway.

I'm still not really sure what she meant. But I guess it doesn't matter, because she seems content to move on to talking about how bad everyone else drives, as she weaves carefully between the lanes trying to get past the more energy-efficient vehicles.

I stare out at the passing landscape and agree with everything she says so she won't tell me more uncomfortable truths about myself.

Emma takes an exit into the plastic, family-friendly Hellscape of Orange County—Irvine, I think. I don't know what day it is but the traffic seems lighter than what I would expect for whatever time of day it is right now.

Consulting some notes in her phone, she takes an illegal left onto a gravel road that I think isn't a road. We rumble along dying grass that, cards played just right, might someday grow into a beautiful wildfire, through the open gate of a tall chain link fence, and into some kind of sunny storage lot. It's filled with huge shipping containers stacked around the area in such a way as to make the interior perfectly private from all prying eyes. Shady. Only metaphorically, of course.

A tall, spindly woman emerges from behind a container, shading her eyes with long, long fingers. She's sporting a kind of working-woman's jumpsuit that's as much stain as not and the kind of edgy, haphazard haircut that lets everyone around know that she's into licking pussy.

Emma watches the stranger for a long moment, doing the math in her head. Grabbing her purse from the backseat and climbing out of the vehicle, she says to me, "Stay in the car."

I'm sure she already knew that my master plan all along has been to chill here and not move my legs even a little.

Have you heard the one about Mr. Fudge and the penguin's car?

Mr. Fudge is a mechanic who owns his own little shop on the bad side of town. On one slow day, around noon, a penguin brings his car in complaining about a strange noise. Having nothing pressing on his plate, Mr. Fudge gets to work right away.

He apologizes to the penguin for not having a waiting room, and recommends that he hang out at the ice cream shop across the street to avoid trouble with any number of seedy characters in the area. The penguin grumbles at this but does ultimately leave, saying he'll be back soon.

After about half an hour, the penguin returns. He asks, "Have you figured out the issue?"

Mr. Fudge looks up from the engine and says, "Looks like you blew a seal."

"Mind your fucking business," the penguin says, wiping his mouth. "I asked about my car."

Emma talks to the lesbian beanpole briefly, then fishes around in her purse and produces a small paper bundle, all tied up with twine. They then talk for much longer. It looks like they're arguing. Haggling, maybe. The bundle goes back into the purse. The lady touches Emma's arm and she pulls away. I still can't tell what she's saying out there, but she's certainly saying it loudly.

I ought to go out and be the big, strong man who settles this. Then again, Emma told me to stay in the car. And she insisted on being taller than me, after all.

Yelling seems to resolve the disagreement, though. Mommy Long-Legs puts her hands up and backs off, says something with a conciliatory expression on her spidery face, then pulls a wad of cash out of her pocket.

The bundle reemerges and is curtly traded for the cash. Emma quickly leafs through the money, nodding to herself, and then exchanges a few last words—sharp words, from the looks of it, with a finger point and even a cranky little stomp—before heading back to the car.

That sure looked like a drug deal. I don't really see what all this has to do with saving the world, unless Emma's involved with some federal agencies. The buyer dips back into the container labyrinth, to either get high or save the world.

"That sure looked like a drug deal," I say when Emma gets back into the car.

Her ethnic ranting ends with a low, "Fucking dyke…"

"What?" Did she mean me?

"Bitch tried to fuck me instead of paying."

"I knew it."

"What?"

"Lesbian. I called it."

"Whatever."

"Was that a drug deal?"

"Shut up," she replies as she turns the key in the ignition.

"*That's* what we had to make a stop for?"

Emma sighs in that way she has, like she's just trying to get through the night so she can tell my parents that she'll never watch me again. "I don't need your fucking judgment, Jace. Okay? Angela asked me to make a few drops on the way and—guess what—people like getting high. It would be great if nobody did but I can't stop them. They would just find it somewhere else. What did you think the '*secret magical underworld*' would be? It's just fucked up people getting fucked up. Any sane person could've predicted that... Besides, it's not *technically* a drug. More of a... an enchantment, I guess."

Didn't she say that her mom died from drugs?

"Fuck off, Jace."

"I didn't say anything!"

"I can see your shitty thoughts all over your face."

But when I look at her, Emma's not seeing me at all. She's staring off at a faded pink shipping container. I didn't know pink made shipping containers.

"I wasn't thinking anything... I just—how about trick peas? Does she sell those?"

"I don't know. Probably. Yes. Look. I just deliver the pizzas."

"Pizza?"

"Are you being stupid on purpose?"

"Why can't she do it herself?"

"Why doesn't the chef bring the pizza to your door? She's busy. And I handle risk better."

"Were we at *risk* here?"

"There's always *some* risk, in anything you do. But I can understand you not knowing that, since you spend all day sitting at a computer in a dark room. But don't worry. I have a good instinct for this sort of thing. A woman's intuition. I just skip a drop if it feels off."

"I bet. Does she at least pay you?"

"Obviously. You think I'd do this for free? I get a reasonable cut."

"Do I get a reasonable cut for being in danger alongside you?"

"Fuck off," she says, but in an affectionate sort of way. She throws the car into reverse and starts turning around to leave. I hope I do get a cut. It doesn't have to be cash. I'll take a handjob and a can of baked beans. Just *something*.

"Are there more?"

"Um..." She halts mid-K-turn and looks down to consult a list on her phone. "Three more in Orange County, one out in the desert, and the last is in Arizona."

"Way the Hell out there?"

"Yeah. That one's weird. I've gone as far as Fresno, though. I think that's not too much different."

I pretend I know where that is. "Is it even worth going that far?"

"If the price is right, sure," Emma says, as she bounces us slowly back over the gravel not-a-road. "Plus, it's on the way this time. To Kansas."

"Alabama."

"Italy."

Emma pulls over almost immediately after we get back to real road and gets out to make a phone call. I watch her standing on the sidewalk, one hand on her hip, making her mystery call in private.

She's right not to trust me. I tell her so when she gets back in and she calls me a jackass, but she laughs as she says it so it's alright.

Emma uses her phone to look up directions to the next stop, which is a squat house in an awful, copy-pasted, middle-upper class neighborhood. She decides after studying the house from a distance to skip it. She offers no explanation, even though I do ask.

She drives some distance before pulling over again. This time, the phone call is much longer and, at least from where I'm sitting, more agitated. I bet she's in trouble for skipping that one.

They appear to reach some kind of agreement by the end of the call. Emma stays standing outside after hanging up, looking down at the sidewalk with hands on hips.

I'm starting to get bored. I rummage around in the glove compartment and look through the CDs. I don't recognize any of these artists. Better luck next time, Emma.

Have you heard the one about Mr. Fudge and the penguin's car?

It's a different penguin.

This other penguin brings his car into Mr. Fudge's shop and complains that it's making a horrible grinding noise.

Mr. Fudge says, "Have you tried removing the Death Grips CD?"

I lied. I recognize that one.

The penguin screams into the void.

The next time I look up, she's on the phone again, walking toward the driver side door. She hangs up as she grabs the handle but I do manage to make out, muffled but distinct, "Such a bitch."

I hope I'm not the bitch. Sometimes I can be, but I like to think I'm just a little sassy.

Emma climbs in and sits for a long moment. She looks tired. I think the phone was too heavy.

"Good call?"

She gives me a look. Then she turns away, sighs, and comes back with a nicer look. Resting a hand on my arm, she says, "Danny says, 'Hi.'"

"Does he really?"

"Well, he asked how you're doing. Same thing."

"Did he *really*?"

"Yeah!"

"What did he call me?"

Emma takes her hand back and starts the car. She says, "Nothing worse than what I call you."

I guess that's good enough.

The next drop is to the shortest non-midget I've ever seen. We find the burly little fucker meditating on a sandy sidewalk in Huntington Beach, humming along with the tune of crashing waves. He's sporting sunglasses and rags and a big, friendly beard. He must be a very cunning Dwarf indeed to have evaded the endless game of homeless relocation that the rich crackers and noodles play as they keep shoving their trash into neighboring municipalities.

Emma's mood immediately brightens upon seeing him, which is a little suspicious if you ask me. She knows him by name, and says it as she calls out to him. It sounds weird and long so I immediately forget it.

His voice is bottomless and his greeting the sun. This stocky monster smiles and nods toward me, and exudes such warmth that I could almost understand if Emma were to dump me for him. Almost.

The exchange—a tied-off plastic bag for a smaller one of cloth—goes pleasantly, without a single raised voice or sexual advance.

Emma clearly already knew him; their conversation is relaxed and flows easily. I don't know what kind of relationship they have, but I'm left wondering if, sexual advance or not, I'm competing in her mind against this dude's probable monster cock. Is it even legal with a Dwarf? I'm afraid to ask about it.

I stand around as they chat in that normal, easy way people have that makes me a little angry. I know it shouldn't—shut up.

Have you heard the one about the slow dwarf?

This joke went over his head.

I zone back in.

Emma and the Dwarf are sharing bits of gossip, laughing about how crummy her bag looks compared to his, and asking each other about people I've never met. They laugh and laugh and I stand here watching them.

At least I'm taller than him.

Eventually, they wrap up their bullshit and that chode of a man briskly walks away on his quick, stumpy legs. Emma arches a silent eyebrow at me before leading us back to the car. What does that mean? It probably means that she's going to dump me on the side of the road and go back to his sex tunnel.

"Was that a Dwarf?"

"Yeah."

"*Really?*"

"Yes! Stop acting shocked by everything. They exist. They're pretty cool."

"So, you and he are good friends?"

"*She.*"

"Bullshit."

"I'm serious."

"With that big fucking beard?" And monster cock?

"That's what they're like, Jace. She's really sweet. You shouldn't be such a dick."

"It's just... Fucking ridiculous, that they're *exactly* like Tolkien. Like this was all made up by a 12-year-old fan-fiction writer."

"Other way around. Tolkien was the 12-year-old."

Oh.

"But remember," Emma continues. "If you ever meet one and actually *talk*, they don't really like the comparison. Kind of like how we don't say, 'witch.' Stereotypes, negative connotations, you know."

"What do you say, then?"

She stops and looks back at me, shading her eyes from the sun. "Talk to them like a normal person, you jackass."

"I mean, can you call them Dwarves?"

"It's not what *they* say, but they usually don't mind."

"What do they say?"

"Just... People."

"Oh."

"They don't really get caught up in all the race bullshit. Not the ones I've met, at least."

"Oh."

"Yep."

"Are Elves real?"

"I think so. Never met one myself, but Angela says she knows a few."

"Oh. You kind of look like an Elf."

"Shut up. I don't."

"Are dragons real?"

"I don't know. Plenty of stories, obviously, but most people I know think they're a myth. The conspiracy theorists think they're extinct."

"What's the conspiracy?"

"What?"

"Conspiracy theorists, right? What conspiracy killed all the dragons? Was it Klaus Schwab?"

"Who?"

"I don't know. Why aren't dragons real?"

"I don't know how to answer that."

"Dwarves aren't a myth, or Elves. How can dragons be, with all the stories?"

"Maybe they actually are extinct. You'd notice a dragon flying around, right?"

Maybe I wouldn't. Maybe we can dig up some bones.

"Are Dwarves masters of earth magic?"

"That's not how magic works."

"How *does* it work?"

Emma looks at me, and then out to sea. "I don't know," she admits. "Just... not like that. There's no earth element."

"How can you say it's not like that when you don't know what it's like?"

She doesn't answer. We get into the car and I ask why she doesn't use magic more, and if she has more than just the marbles. I also ask about unicorns, leprechauns, and the Dutch. But Emma ignores me to send a text and pull up directions to the next drop.

Following the phone woman's instructions, we make our way to a busy shopping plaza. Snooty shops enclose a massive central lot with tiny, green-painted parking spots that you can barely see against the asphalt.

Emma parks the car near a fruity juice affair filled to the brim with the same. She stares intensely at the small manicured gardens and benches and all the people milling about them.

"Why would you drug-deal in such a crowded—"

"Shut up," Emma snaps. But she doesn't even say it fun. "Go for a walk."

"I didn't do anything."

"*Shut the fuck up,*" she hisses, pushing her palms into her temples and breathing vicious little Cuban curses that I don't know.

"What's your—"

"Get out! Get the fuck out of my car."

It sounds like she means it. I don't know what to do in the face of this genuine, not-even-funny anger. We stare at each other. Her face is flushed, her breath ragged and animal. I try to think of something I can say. To *that* face?

"Now!" she screams. "Get out!"

I don't know what to do. I don't understand what's happening. Why is she so mad? I didn't even try to lesbian seduce her. She keeps yelling but I'm not really hearing it anymore. I get out of the car, leaving all my stuff behind in the backseat. I glance back after a moment to see if she'll change her mind but she's not even looking. Why do people always treat me like this?

Fuck.

Have you heard the one about the Russian and his sentence?

Rodion, guilty and convicted of axe murder, is sent to Siberia for hard labor. He's added to the end of a chain gang swinging picks and shovels to break the icy earth, a task with truly no point but to break backs. However, due to the nature of his crimes, Rodion isn't permitted any tools that could be used as weapons against the guards.

"This is outrageous," Rodion cries to the guards, presumably in Russian, if you go in for that sort of thing. "How am I to work with no tools? I may as well return to Saint Petersburg and continue on with my life if you've no suitable punishment for me."

The guards, bemused, look out at the endless expanse of frozen nothing and shrug. They turn to Rodion, grinning, and suggest he kick rocks.

I shove my hands into my pockets and get started on a shuffling lap of the plaza, with all its pruned palm trees and repulsive crowds. Maybe Emma will still be here when I come back around. Maybe she'll leave a pile of my shit on the sidewalk and tap dance into the sunset. Maybe I'll get struck by lightning twice and die of axe murder.

Turning the first corner, I have to squeeze twice through an endless queue of people waiting to get into a pancake spot of some kind. I stop to trace the line's zigs and zags and silly spirals around the tables of early bird outdoor diners eating their stupid pancakes with their stupid fucking mimosas. No cake, pan or otherwise, is worth such indignity.

Farther down that next side, I'm accosted by a small, shriveled Asian woman in a thick winter coat, even though it must be at least 70°F (112°C). She barks something at me in what I recognize as Korean but can't really understand on account of my not actually knowing the language.

I ask, "What?"

I hope she repeats it in English because otherwise I'm not going to catch it the second time.

The woman sighs in theatrical disgust. She rolls her dumb, squinty eyes and walks away, ranting to a gaggle of similarly post-menopausal women of the same race and general temperament. They take no care to keep their voices down but, of course, they know I don't understand.

I do, though. I don't need to know what they're saying to know what they're fucking saying. Without responding, I turn and continue on. They continue mocking me in Korean.

I stare at the dark side walk. I am a storm cloud, creeping black threat, rumble-bellied. I see no crowd as I blow down from darkest Heaven. They can move out of *my* path. They can give ground to *me*. For once.

Scum, all of them. The one group of people you'd expect to treat us right and they're the worst of all. As it's always fucking been, right? And all I could ever do in retaliation was deny myself, withdraw and kill the lights and vanish for good. As if they'd ever care.

Fuck them.

I'm big as the sky, as terrible, as fey. I'll tear down the earth and whirlwind it away. All light will sputter and choke in my torrential rebuke. Upon my cyclone be broken in your attempts at abuse.

Something suddenly wraps tight around me. I look down and the black cloud of anger disperses into smoky tendrils to reveal a pair of long, white arms crossing over my chest.

I unclench my jaw. I uncurl my balled fists and let my arms hang at my sides.

What was I about to do?

Probably nothing. I don't even know how to do anything. Always the thunder but never a strike.

I look up and see that I've stormed past the car and around to the pancake line again. Still holding me from behind, Emma brings her head forward next to mine.

"Dumdum," she says softly, in way that I think I'm meant to understand is an apology.

"It's just a lot," she says softly. It is, but I don't know what she means.

I don't think that's what I was mad about.

Still, something in me flares electric, tiny and muted, shrouded in the blurred grayness at the bottom of a deep, deep well. I can't quite tell what it is. I can't tell if I'm better. I can't tell. But it feels nice to be held anyway.

A raindrop breaks upon Emma's arm. Above us, the sky's face darkens.

The scenery morphs slowly as we crawl east on I-40. Far, far behind us, a dark blotch on the horizon, distant flashes of lightning tiptoeing over a small area of soaked plastic. Ahead and around us, the arid hills look faintly alien. The vegetation is brittle and lifeless. We pass occasionally between squat, red and tan cliffs where the highway simply blasts through a hill rather than going over or around.

The last drop was some spy movie shit, with a latitude and longitude instead of an address, because there was no address. All we found was an honor system false rock a short walk off the road.

We acted honorably, of course. I joked about acting otherwise, but Emma said it was too risky; she declined to explain further.

Late afternoon sunrays of tarnished yellow paint the most intricate designs on the dashboard. The sky's a deep, monotone blue, unblemished from horizon to horizon. Except for that one tiny speck of anger, of course, way behind us, hovering over a glorified strip mall full of insufferable old Korean women.

Aside from a single truck far ahead of us, there's no one else out here. This bright desolation must stretch for hundreds of miles in every direction. It must, for it to be so complete, for it to so completely drive out any hint of real life.

It's easy, looking at such a landscape as this, with all its nothing spread out to the farthest edges of nothing, to imagine yourself as the last living person left. Too easy. Too self-important, overwhelmingly melancholic. Too typical a notion to be true. Don't you think so?

Imagine a luminous tapestry of silver threads, a gleaming, glowing network of souls emerging into a collective consciousness of brilliance. I think I can see it. It fills the sky. It hangs like wavering sword points on high.

Imagine a neuron falling silent, growing dim and fading into the primal darkness that rushes in when a thread snaps. Maybe patterns on the cortex are broken and they wink out.

Maybe they don't. Maybe they effortlessly rearrange or—God, oh, God, I pray not—maybe they don't even notice.

Maybe the orphaned neuron is immersed and lost in a dream about himself, alone and damned, too busy, too sadly determined to realize he fell. Spellbound, defenseless, never to be saved. Unnoticed as he slips under the waves.

Isn't that the sad part—that there's no context at all? I think, I feel that too. Maybe. I don't know.

"Stop staring out the window like that," she says.

"What?"

"You haven't said anything for an hour."

I look at Emma and find her staring at me. I gesture toward the windshield.

"Shit!" Her eyes snap back to the road, and then flicker back and forth between me and it. Safe. Although, if I'm being fair, things are mostly straight and clear around here.

"You haven't said anything for over an hour."

"Oh. Sorry." After a moment, I add, "I'm not mad."

She rolls her eyes, taking us two ocular shifts removed from eyes on the road. "I *know* you're not mad. I'm not sure you even have the emotional capacity to *be* mad." The smirk, the eyebrow. "Just give me some attention."

"Okay. Um..." I should talk about something interesting. Maybe the lights?

"Oh my god," Emma mutters, not really giving me a chance to come up with a topic. She asks, "Do you have any family?"

Oh.

"Shit. Sorry. I know about—um—Baby Paulie. But anyone else? Other siblings? Uncles? Third cousins, twice-removed?"

Paulie Baby. You'd think she could remember that much.

"Just call him Paul."

"Paul."

The car's shadow races ahead of us, nosing ahead by an increasing margin and leaving us in our own dark dust.

"Mom died. Cancer. Paul died. Murder."

"Oh." After a pause she ventures a shrunken "sorry…"

"Dad's still in Joliet, as far as I know." A kind of quiet rage bubbles in my chest; it's an unproductive thing, I know, but it feels good in its way, and you can see why one might indulge. "Everyone else is with *him*."

"I'm sorry," she says eventually.

"I *knew* it was your fault. I've always known!"

"What?"

"Nothing. Is it just you and Danny?"

"Just me and Danny."

Just the Cuban raft baby and her half, black brother.

"Have you heard the one about the orphan?"

Emma rolls her eyes again but I can tell she's still listening, and possibly still watching the road. She drives with both hands on the wheel, exactly where they taught us to put them in high school, like a nerd. She glances at me after a moment. "Well?" she finally asks.

"What?"

"You were going to tell a stupid orphan joke?"

"Oh. I've abandoned it."

I watch her face quickly flash to first annoyance, then confusion. Then she bursts out laughing. The car casually slips halfway into the empty lane beside us before she collects herself and jerks us back in line.

"Oh my god. Wow. You know my parents *died*, right?"

"Did they lose control laughing on the highway?"

That one pulls a guffaw from her. Either laughing or sobbing hysterically, she comes to a swerving, distressing stop, overshooting the ample shoulder to land a tire or two in the gravel. Lucky thing, the utter emptiness of this place, huh?

"That shouldn't be funny," she says eventually, catching her breath and wiping away tears. Are we sure she wasn't crying?

Sorry about your parents. "You have a terrible sense of humor."

"Shut up."

"And you're not a very safe driver."

"Well, you'll drive tomorrow and you can finally show me how to be funny. Let's find somewhere to stop for the night. I'm tired."

"Where are we?"

Emma points to a sign, which I have to ask her to decipher for me because I can't make out the words.

"Eight miles to Needles," she reads without complaint or insult, surprising everyone within an eight-mile radius. What's Needles?

Surprising no one, Needles is a town. The kind of desert town that can't afford the luxury of piped-in water for lawns. The kind of desert town where you sit on the curb in a McDonald's parking lot, as far as possible from the splayed-out local junkie, eating ketchupy burgers and watching the sun go down, and then get a crappy room at the first motel you find. The kind of desert town where you watch dumb reality shows and Emma blows you and enthusiastically swallows, probably because she feels guilty for screaming at you earlier, or for all the dead folks behind you, or for something you don't understand, and then she gets up and says, "Fuck you, Jace," and, "You're eating me out next time," which is fine because you like it but you're not sure what you did wrong.

That kind of desert town.

I show them. I hold it up to the camera, to prove it's real. It's real.

It's late, late at night, and quiet, and the apartment is empty save for me and the glowing screen and the cold. It seeps into my room through gaps around the warped windows. The icy tiles numb my bare feet. Three of four light bulbs don't work. The wounds on my arms are almost perfectly symmetrical.

They ask how I'm doing. They welcome me back. They call me a nigger. They tell me to kill myself. They ask what happened to my face. They say I deserved it. They tell me not to do it. They watch.

I say nothing because the show is better this way. They'll make fun of my voice. They'll make fun of how I talk. They'll ask what's wrong.

It's cold, cold and heavy in my hand. I got it from my uncle, knowing that he'll never tell. He congratulated me on no longer being a pussy bitch nigga. He thinks that's an avuncular affection. He thinks I'm going to kill someone. He hopes. I think.

I pop out the cylinder, show them the five empty chambers, show them the four empty chambers. I give it a quick spin. Look, I show them, it works.

I spin it hard and snap it closed with a flick of my wrist.

They tell me to do it. They beg me not to. They call me a liar. They say they'll call the police. They won't come here. No one will.

It's cold and it's heavy. It's cold in my palm, cold against my temple, cold against my finger.

Click.

Ta-da.

I drop it and it clatters on the tile floor.

I don't read the chat.

I'm here all week.

"Jace."

Someone shakes my shoulder. Where the fuck am I?

"Wake up, dummy. You're snoring."

There's the usual grubby ceiling, but now with an alien fan that must have snuck in while I was sleeping. It casts long, menacing, needle-spider shadows in the blue light.

Oh. Yeah. Right. Needles.

I don't snore.

I raise myself up on my elbows. Emma's reclining next to me with her legs crossed. The other bed appears to be for storage. The only source of light is the big TV mounted on the wall.

A leathery, blonde news lady talks about a missing person of some description. Emma switches to some raunchy cartoon I don't recognize, with unnerving squiggly lines and everything looking like balls.

Then it's a comedic game show where the punchline, every time, is the black host's facial expression. I wish I'd thought of that.

Then a different news show face with a different milk carton picture.

Then home shopping for something ugly and turquoise.

Then we backtrack to the different news show face. She says, in a tone both grim and excited for the ratings boost, that there's been another disappearance, this time in a remote college town.

The display switches to a low-quality photo of a chunky, dark-haired woman sitting at a table, smiling uncomfortably in front of a birthday cake. The news lady speculates with subdued glee that this poor young woman—Tabitha Mae London—is dead, even though no remains have been found.

Why doesn't she say where Jorge went? That's what the people want to know. Did this murderer take my only friend? It's suspicious that she won't deny the allegations, if you ask me.

The news lady says that experts say that this may be the latest in a string of disappearances linked to a possible serial killer that experts say is operating throughout the American Southwest.

That, at least, is what the experts are saying.

Her male counterpart asks if that isn't terrible, but sounds like he's asking if it isn't great. They agree that it is one or the other, and assure us that they'll let us know if the experts come up with any new developments.

If the experts are so smart, how come they haven't given this killer a cool nickname? They don't even know where Jorge is. Some experts.

Emma makes a thoughtful kind of grunt and switches to a show where rich people judge poor people. I think this might be the natural order of things.

"You change the channel a lot."

Emma shrugs without looking away from the screen.

I don't like when people worship the television like this. Active, alert, always hunting and hunting for the best programming, instead of just lying there and letting yourself die a little. That's the way it's meant to be experienced.

"I dreamed that I was famous, spun the wheel and nearly gained to greatness."

"What?"

"Nothing. I had a dream."

"Well, you were freaking out in your sleep, so cut it out. No dreaming allowed."

"Was I?"

"Snoring and snorting and kicking. Very annoying," she assures me.

"What time is it?"

"Sleep."

Emma kills the broadcast and tosses the remote onto the storage bed. After some Spanish wrestling and cursing, she manages to pull the taut sheets back from under us. She insists that we need to cover ourselves like normal people.

Once we're cocooned in the blankets to her satisfaction, Emma pulls me close and burrows herself into me. I feel her breath on my neck. I feel her heartbeat against my skin. I feel her lips move as she says, "'Night, stupid. No more dreaming."

I feel something sneaking up on me, in my eyes and nose and chest and throat, and I start peeling her off me so I can go hide my shame in the grimy bathroom.

"Stay," she says, squeezing my ribs a little. "It's fine."

So, I stay. I sniffle a little, trying to keep it down.

I wish I had a reason to be like this.

Emma breathes her loud, deep breaths. She plants a gentle kiss just below the line of my jaw, and—damn it—it makes me a little worse.

Chuckling to herself, shaking the bed, she whispers, "Pussy."

I'm out of my chair, on thin carpet, hobbling. Frankie calls me a horrid little goblin.

I love him.

Someday, I'll find a way to repay him. I hope. If I have the time.

Mum would be furious to know he brought me here. She won't know, of course. We'd never tell her. But if she were to find out, Frankie would kindly instruct her to fuck off.

Good.

Sorry.

I'm sorry, Mum. I know it's hard. I know you try your best to understand, and you try your best not to resent me in the deepest, darkest, most secret and ashamed corner of your heart. I try my best not to let on that I know, not to resent you back, not to be a burden.

I'm trying.

I turned sixteen two days ago. There was a sad cake, with sad candles, and sad singing. I should've died four years ago and counting, if you believe the doctors who did this to me.

Sometimes I think about stepping out myself, just to spare everyone else the trouble. We're all stuck together, and no one asked for this, and no one wants to be the first to say, "I'm done."

I mean, aside from Dad, who was done maybe six or seven years ago—fucking bastard.

Don't think about Dad. Don't think about them. Don't fuck this up.

After pointing out the envelope, Frankie puts in his headphones and says he'll be listening to his heavy metal in the bathroom until we finish. But I know he'll be listening at the door, just in case.

I wish he wouldn't. Earlier, he said he wouldn't, but I think sometimes even he forgets that I understand.

At least he keeps the promises that matter, I guess.

She smiles wide as she comes over to help me up onto the bed. She kisses me—stay cool—and says sweet, sweet things as she unbuttons my shirt. Stay cool. She knows how to move, how to talk, how to look. I can tell this is a real professional. I almost believe her eyes.

"Please don't be scared of me. I can't control it. I'm trying my best," I want to tell her. But I can't; that's the one surefire way to make it worse. As if I could get the words out anyway. Stay cool.

She leaves a lipstick print on my neck, my chest. I try to stay in the moment, knowing that this is my only chance, but I've never had a moment, ever, not with anyone.

I can't help hearing in my head, again and again, after months and after the gifts and the laughing and everything else, "I think we should just be friends." Just once, this isn't a big deal for normal people. I get that. But it's a promise for me, one that will last until the day that I die, and maybe that's soon to be, but I can't spend my whole life being denied.

The moment? I try to will myself calm.

She lets out a gagged squeal when I accidentally smack the back of her head. I'm sorry, I'm sorry, I'm sorry! She comes up for air, tells me it's okay. I'm sorry! She smiles but it's a strained one and a paid-for one and I don't believe it, not for a single second.

Please don't be scared of me. Please don't hate me. I didn't ask to be like this.

The demon in my nerves smacks her again and she climbs off, leaving me dripping onto the bedsheets. I apologize, over and over. I don't beg out loud. But, then, do I have to?

She apologizes, perfunctorily, draws a line—close off, clothes on.

"I'm done," she says.

"I think we should just be friends," she doesn't say, because she doesn't want even that. A professional, through and through. I thought this would be better, but it isn't.

Immediately, Frankie is out, arguing with her. She tries to take the money and get out quickly. He's getting worked up, arguing, shouting. She's trying to force her way past him, spitting vague threats. She *knows* people.

Maybe Frankie's right. Maybe sometimes I *don't* understand. I don't know what the fuck everyone is so *mad* about.

They become a static backdrop, white noise, remote blurs. They fade into the background, and I fade into theirs. If you have to learn, you never forget how to do it.

I look around until I find my clothes on the floor. I could rappel myself down there and get dressed. But I can't bring myself to move.

So, I sit here, on an unfamiliar bed, twisted cripple, naked, drooping, leaking fluids.

No one wants to fuck the broken boy, the damaged boy, the pitiable, not-even-pity fuck. Not with his corkscrew spine and his nervous devil and his crooked retard arms. Not even for money.

They can't even be near him.

I already knew this. Sometimes they can admit it, quietly to themselves, and maybe even out loud when pressed, drunk, trashy, vicious. Either way, I hear it. Always.

Why do they have to keep telling me—I know! —again and again and again?

I crawl to the edge of the bed. My boxers are on the ground. Everyone's fighting.

Why are they so mad?

Why did Frankie bring me here?

I'm falling.

I hit the floor, and there goes my breath.

For a moment, I stay there, tangled in the sheets, eyes half-glued closed, gasping into the thin, patterned carpet under my cheek. There's a kind of comfort to this. Even this. As long as I don't move.

But I do.

Unraveling myself, I sit up to find Emma kneeling on the bed, eyes wide and hands over her mouth. "Ow," I inform her.

"Sorry."

"Did you do that on purpose?"

"I didn't think you'd land that hard."

I climb back onto the bed. I say, "I dreamed I was…"

"Not interested. We have to check out in half an hour."

…broken and dysfunctional, and set out to find just how unlovable…

"Jace! Get up!"

…Okay.

I get up, but slowly. Emma escorts me roughly to the bathroom, tugging my shirt over my head as we go. Once I'm successfully bounced up to the shower, she twists the knob to a boil, pantses and lightly gropes me, and leaves me to my scalding.

"Make it quick," she calls back to me. "We have to check out soon."

I make it quick, even though I do spend some time thinking about last night. I know she was just having a giggle, but does she actually think I'm a pussy? How did she figure it out? If I don't get my shit together, will she simply dip out when I'm not looking? Is she mid-outward-dip right now?

Have you heard the one about the lady who took a dip in the hotel pool?

It took several days and a metric ton of chips to clear the filters of queso.

When I finish up and pull the shower curtain back, I see on the counter a set of clothes folded and left for me, with a complimentary bag of chips placed on top. I dress and wait until I get over the gesture before I leave the bathroom munching on chips.

Emma's looking out the window into the parking lot, phone held up to her ear. She brings it down, taps at the screen, listens again. She alternates between fingers and ear several times. She swears under her breath. Turning, she throws the phone down onto the storage bed.

She smiles when she sees me. Maybe everything's alright.

She looks tired. I tell her so, and I realize immediately that this is a mistake. She gives me a look that confirms it. Why didn't you stop me from being an asshole?

"You can really be an asshole sometimes, Jace."

"I-I meant, you know, I'm concerned."

"I know," she sighs, turning back to her duffel bag. "Finish your breakfast, stupid. Brush your teeth. We have to head out."

Squinting more than usual, I try to see if the dim sign ahead indicates that we're nearing Flagstaff. Emma didn't say how long it would take.

"Just follow the freeway until we get to Flagstaff," she said.

"Easy," she said, right before curling up like a cat and falling sound asleep.

It's weird that she calls a highway a freeway.

After closing the distance, I see that the sign says, "Las Vegas". That doesn't sound right.

I look over at Emma cat-napping against the door. She'll be mad if I wake her. She'll be mad if she finds out that I don't have a license. She'll be mad if we end up in Las Vegas. Or will she? Maybe she likes craps? I could drop a load myself. What about the Nazis?

I can probably figure this out. Right?

Have you heard the one about the sage's wrong turn?

A Tibetan monk goes on vacation and takes a tour of Mexico. On his long flight back home, he decides to meditate to pass the time. But the monk meditates so hard that he transcends to another plane, and is shocked to find himself landing in Albuquerque.

Albuquerque must be somewhere around here too, right? What if I try to go to Las Vegas and take a wrong turn and end up enlightened? Travel is hard.

The next sign I can make out says, "Holy Moses Wash". Washington? Which one? Is one better? Moses? What the fuck.

The next: "Slow vehicles ahead".

The noble city of Slow Vehicles Ahead, AZ. It's not where I'm trying to be, but at least we're no longer lost, and Emma will never have to know. I keep going.

As we pass through another nameless desert town full of desert people and their desert lives, the car radio starts losing its focus on where we started. First the voices get tinny, then a rising tide of static and snowstorm starts creeping in, then, finally, the speakers produce a steady ocean drone, with here and there whispers of the drowned.

It's annoying. I turn it off altogether and drive in silence.

In the following void of sound, I find there is no void. There's the soft rumble of tire and asphalt asking each other riddles. There's the roar of wind being torn and reshaped around the vehicle. There's my breath, and my heart, and a thousand other treasonous signs of my moving parts.

There's me and Emma and Emma's red sedan. There's a truck being passed by an old beige van. There are huge spans of dry vegetation and mountains behind them, eroded by distance. There's the road, long and uniform and hypnotic and sleepy and…

Shit! I snap my eyes back to the road. What happened?

I could've killed us.

But, on the other hand, everything's fine. I'm still following the pavement and the painted lines; I'm still keeping near the speed limit; the minutes and miles are passing quietly beneath us. Soon I find a sign that says it's 99 miles to Flagstaff, which I'm fairly certain is closer than when we started. Everything's fine.

I screw up my eyes to read the next mile marker but can't make it out. Why's it getting so dark out? Emma's car insists that it's early afternoon, but red has been known to lie to me in the past. It certainly doesn't look like half-past-one.

The world is enveloped in strange, blinding shadows, like the flashbang afterimage when you go inside suddenly on a bright day. Everything around me is shrouded in its own personal dusk. I navigate between dark islands in a sea of light.

At the farthest reaches of the world as I know it, across countless leagues of tan and muddy greens, beneath heavy, ragged clouds squatting darkly on the horizon, there sit the mountains, shimmering in the weird light, hunched over to protect their secrets beyond.

I imagine walking forever across the plains—or running it in a third of forever—and scrambling up to peek my head finally over the last crag. And I imagine a paradise, a covert, a perfect place. A peace. I imagine a peace, a shelter and balm for the soul, a bodiless love flowing out of absence.

It's a place where no human foot has ever trodden, and that's the source of its beauty, and my blighted step is the one to turn it all to Hell, and—no. Maybe not that.

Maybe I imagine God, or Something Akin, is living in that valley. And He imagines me, pilgrimaging up the slopes on hands and bloody knees. And He imagines that I'll get to the proper point and stop, turn back, go free.

Maybe I'll imagine Him into reality, when the time comes, and He'll imagine me back. Maybe we dream together, and we're as real as we make each other. Maybe those unreal, unrealized places are the locus for all reality.

Stupid. It's so tempting to try to create reality, to shape it through sheer force of will. Does that ever work? I can't imagine it does, not for me.

I just want to think that something great is in there, in those voids. And I'm real. And you. Is that so bad? Can you really blame me? I wouldn't blame you. You know I don't.

Have you heard the one about the world's greatest surgeon?

He—

Emma gasps and lets out a little squeak.

I thought she was sleeping. I look at her and she's pressed back against the window, away from me, her chest heaving.

What?

She looks terrified. What happened?

"What?"

She slowly lowers herself into her seat, but keeps me in front of her. As if I were the crazy one.

Rude? No. It's something, to me, but it's not rude. What did I do?

"I have to pee," she breathes.

The mouse trap handle snaps finally. I rattle the nozzle in the car's gas hole to shake out the last few drops, being careful not to exceed the recommended number of shakes lest it look like I'm playing with it.

Still, on the way back to the holster I leave a sparse trail of gasoline drips along the pavement and in my underpants. I should've played with it.

Instead of the usual brightly colored velocity mart or some such thing, this gas station has a trading post. There's an Indian feel to it—*heya hoya*, not curry—with a strong theme of logs, bears, elk, and wagon wheels. An animatronic noble savage in a glass box harasses customers as they walk in.

I can't tell if all this decoration is racist. If it is, it's at least a charming sort of racism. There's a certain warmth to it when seen through a fog of your own breath.

As soon as we arrived, Emma dashed into the trading post to trade her pee for provisions. It must have been quite urgent. But maybe they're upselling her to a poo now, as she's been in there a while. Hopefully, she doesn't blow everything on glass beads. It's a real danger out here on the frontier, bead addiction.

I think she's mad but she said she wasn't when I asked. What can I do? Was I supposed to ask again? A third time? What's the right number of times? Is it that time of the month?

I check the date on my phone. December 18th. That explains it. It must be her time of December. That's probably why she's mad.

A minivan with too many people in it angrily inches by to get to the gas pump in front of me. It takes a couple of back-and-forths to get properly situated.

The minivan is white. White makes cars for girls. Nobody in the family says anything about the white but the driver, when he steps out, turns out to be a bald, angrily glaring man.

Maybe he's mad that he has a girl car. It must be his time of the month too.

To avoid further menstrual glares and muttered racial slurs, I move Emma's car out of the way to an actual parking spot.

And then I wait.

And wait.

Maybe she's sick?

I look at my phone.

And wait.

I tap the arrow keys through my seven contacts, half of them dead, and loop around and around until I settle on Jorge. I stare at it for a long time before pressing the button to call.

It rings and rings and rings until a robot woman starts saying something I don't let her finish. It's pretty out of character for Jorge to let the fembot take a call.

I tap further and call the homeless shelter, but I don't know what I'm hoping to accomplish here. A curt woman answers and tells me that there is no one named Jorge there, and then that there is no one named Savannah there. I almost ask for Anne Frank, but catch myself before I say something that would make her look at me funny.

I tried. Right? You saw.

Shut up.

My ass hurts. Damn it.

When I get out of the car to stretch, I hear a commotion from the far end of the stone-paved walkway that stretches across the building's face.

Well, I've got nothing better to do, right? I walk over to check it out.

The stone slabs become dusty asphalt, and then sunbaked gravel, though I imagine they haven't been baked in earnest for weeks. There's some kind of street performer, or mad scientist, settled into the center of a haphazard assortment of trash and instruments. It's somewhere between a Rube Goldberg machine and post-apocalyptic refuge. It's somewhere between music and insanity.

It's somewhere, in any case.

Is it? Here?

A street performer, here, at a just-off-the-highway trading post, barely a street to perform on, with nothing but on-ramps and the resting bodies of injured trucks. Of all the places in, over, or under the world where he could possibly be…

I sidle up to the edges of the small, scattered crowd of itinerants watching him. The hat on the ground contains a few bills, but I don't see anyone drop anything in.

The man is large, bearded, with dark eyes and dark thoughts. His hat and his voice are anachronistic, apologetic. His oversized coat of black and white checks makes him a rumbling mountain of volume and chess ski slopes.

Leaning back in a rusted metal folding chair, he strums a guitar with a four-fingered hand. With violent boots, he stomps and crashes various drums, symbols, and loosely percussive garbage. Ignoring the harmonica affixed to a brace around his neck, he belts, mourns, raps, roars, rages a song like an absurd hymn of damnation.

There's a faint sense of danger in the air, of furious threat turned inward. It weaves a spell that rises up over me. There's the song, and in a haze the singer and the listener. Everything else turns unreal as I lose track of the audience, the site, the sky, the light.

In the tune, I see a man apart, with something he desperately needs to say and no one to listen. I see a symphony of blood sport, arcs of the stuff across the face of stage and fan alike when curtains close. The laughter and laughter and sickening laughter that races you to the cobblestones, because you didn't catch on in time which parts of the act were for entertainment purposes only.

His lyrics are cryptic, derisive and self-referential but it's a secret. It's an exhausted metaphor. He thinks it's clever but he's terrified and spiraling into incomprehensibility. I look into the music man's blackened heart and hate it, fucking hate the rotting pieces of it that mirror my own...

But his ridiculous music is beautiful, and terrible, and it makes me want to descend into the cave and dynamite the mouth behind me. It does things to a soul, things both tender and savage. It crawls into the roots of your being and it caresses, tears, rips, repairs, again and again, ravaging and restoring, again and again.

Have you heard the one about the one-man band?

This one, you must, *must* know:

There was a music man, and he was so, so tired of being alone. So, he formed a band. It was just him, and too many instruments, and a microphone, and that's all.

And he worked together with himself to produce, against all odds and expectation, a melody and poem to achieve divinity.

And, finally, the culmination of a bit of cosmic, fucking cosmic hilarity, I reduced this piece of Heaven down to an ungodly, graceless, fucking stupid punchline.

In any case, the one-man band broke up, due to creative differences.

God damn—another one of God's bad jokes.

I'm terrified to look. But it'll get me if I look away. Eyes resolutely on a safe patch of nothing on the pavement, I watch the man-shadow from my periphery. It watches me back. It looks just like me. It seeks my gaze and pulls at it, as it pulls at everything.

Reality is warping all around me. It sucks at the eye. Everyone else is gone. It's just me and the dark beast, just me. My surroundings fade to colorless, to murk, to nothing. Everything gone. Even the pavement and the safe patch of nothing and the sky and the sun.

I continue wailing—what else can I do? I could sing about hope. I could sing about the sun in my eyes on a cool blue morning. But I don't. I didn't. I spent my whole life raging and raging against the night, shouting into the abyss, praying that it would awaken the angels. And now I've sung breath into a night I'd thought forever lifeless. And it looks *just* like me. I wish I could take that life back, into myself. Oh, God! I'm sorry! I'm sorry, but what else can I do?

The somber dragon grows and grows, out of my own throat, blotting out the world and becoming the world and wrapping itself sleepily all around me. This is mine. This is me. I did this. A lazy tail of writhing shadow drapes over my neck. It flicks another loop.

I cry out for someone to come and save me, for the first time in my life.

The beast cries out for someone to come and save me. It stares with veiled eyes. It pulls. It claps. It yawns. It wraps. It fills my lungs with darkness and it pulls, pulls at my heart.

Something flickers in front the beast as it sings. A tiny mote of light struggles impossibly against the infinite strength of the beast's gravity. I see now how it arcs around and around in a collapsing orbit. I hear, beneath my own crooning, the faint sound of wings.

The faint sound of wings, from behind my right shoulder. A dim glow dancing across the contours of my face.

I try to turn my neck to find the halo.

The loop tightens.

Everyone's gone.

There are still the travelers, going about their various rest stop duties, but the musician and the crowd are gone. The whole mad scientist machine is gone. The dragon is gone.

Dragon? Emma said those aren't real.

I scramble to my feet and wipe the dust off my clothes. The sky is a quarter burned to ash by now, cloudless throughout except on the deathbed horizon, where the billows stack to a mountain of pillows crowned by a pastel kingdom.

What happened? Did I fall asleep out here? Did they just leave me here?

The pink and yellow king of clouds, way the fuck off at the edge of the world, whispers something about skies and dust and laughter but I don't listen.

I dreamed I spent a lifetime seeking grace and found it only when I gave up the chase.

I don't tell the king about it.

Where's Emma?

Did they fucking leave me here?

Did she?

I light a cigarette so it doesn't look so weird that I'm just standing here. Leaning against the foundation to an elk statue at the edge of the lot, there's a dark little woman. She's wizened and bundled and clearly stoned out of her fucking gourd with divine madness. She looks the type to be completely phased out of existence, invisible and unseeing, but she stares at me hard.

I puff, puff, puff and check my phone to avoid her gaze. Still December 18th. So, it hasn't been that long, after all. But I should go look for Emma anyway. Maybe she fell in. Or maybe she's been looking for me. Maybe I just don't like being noticed by crazy old ladies like this.

I give the woman one last covert glance. Thankfully, she's no longer digging at me with her spaced out irises. Her head is turned toward the cloud king. As if that blowhard has anything interesting to say.

I don't know what I'm talking about. Whatever. I turn away.

I stop outside the entrance to the trading post. Of course, she's not inside. I just know, somehow. It's a feeling in the gut, or the spinal cord, or the fundament. Somewhere. Don't you feel it? I think I do. I think she's gone.

I head inside anyway to do a bit of my own trading. There's a short line in the restroom but it moves fast. I slide into a just vacated stall and find that the previous man didn't flush. He was white. Typical.

I piss on his piss to teach him a lesson; this makes me the alpha. It's a doggie dog world out there, you know. Of course, I do flush, because there's a line of eager betas behind me too.

I check quickly down the aisles of counterfeit beaver pelts, small pox blankets, and single-serving potato chip bags, but no Emma. Obviously, I knew I wouldn't find her in here, but it doesn't hurt to check. Maybe I was hoping I'd be wrong. Maybe I was wondering why they have rocks for sale. Maybe I need to keep looking and looking so I don't have to stop looking.

I head outside and shuffle off to check around the corner of the wide building. The world seems less festive on this side. There are dumpsters now. There are fat little propane tanks now. There are Jaces now, dumpy and cold, shuffling along with pockets full of hands. Without the façade of wilderness decorations and warm trading post glows, this is just some gas station with some gift shop, serving some truck drivers who got ass-sore on some boring stretch of highway.

On the far side of a big cluster of dumpsters, there she is, clear as day when nothing else is. I can barely make out anything else at that distance, but there she is. She's folded down in a hobo squat against the backcountry wall of the trading post, cradling something in her arms and staring blankly at the stones.

Emma doesn't look up as I approach.

"So, goodbye forever?"

"Fuck you," she rasps at me dully. Makeup is smeared down her cheeks. She sniffles a big, wet sniffle.

"I—what? What happened?"

What happened? Is it the time of the month? Is it still the 18th? What's she got in her arms?

"Go away."

I stop out of reach. "No—Emma, what happened?"

She doesn't respond. Her gaze drifts away, as if her whole spirit is drifting away. I follow her eyes but it's only empty hills and telephone poles and highway and more empty hills. She sniffs.

"Are we just giving up on the Nazi mission?"

"Fucking hell, Jace! There *are* no fucking Nazis, you mongoloid."

"What?"

"I made it up! When was the last time you saw an actual Nazi? I'm serious—do you have a condition? Are you brain damaged?"

"You lied? Why?"

"So you wouldn't fucking kill yourself!"

But I'm not...

Quieter, she adds, "I thought it would help for you to have a—a purpose. Some reason to stick around. So you're not just drifting aimlessly to suicide."

"I'm not going to—why Nazis?"

"First thing that came to mind. I honestly didn't think you'd even ask."

"I'm not suicidal."

"Yes, you are. I can tell. I'm an empath."

"Bullshit. Everyone says that. And they're always the most self-absorbed people in the world."

"No, Jace. Like, for real. An actual, capital-E Empath."

"What?"

"Magic. Just like you wanted, Jace. You should be thrilled... You know, when we met, that first night at the coffee shop... Do you think that I approach every random man I run into in the dark? You really think that's normal? I could tell you were... Well, harmless. To me, at least."

Didn't she say that she wasn't an artist? Harmless? "Really? You read minds?"

"I just... feel emotions. When I'm near people. And yours..." The fire is gone from her voice; she's all cold again. "It's muted, black... Empty, kind of, but there's still something there, weird and... I don't know. Weird. I can tell, okay? I've felt this before. And they were all..."

"I'm really not suicidal, though. I'm not going to kill myself, Emma. I swear."

"You feel like it. I know that feeling."

What the fuck.

"So, you thought—you thought I was going to *kill* myself. And your solution was to *prank* me. This whole bullshit trip… You sure fooled that dumb fucking fool, Jace. Nazis, fate of the world, drug deals. A thousand and one miles. Just for me. You just—"

I almost suggest that she fucked me as a panacea. But I don't want to find out if that's true.

What the fuck.

Emma takes a deep, shuddering breath, but doesn't say anything.

She said this has happened before. Oh.

I ask, "How many times have you done this?"

She doesn't answer. That many times.

"How many?"

That many.

"How many vulnerable people have you killed?"

"I didn't kill anyone!" she snaps. "I tried to *save* them. I'm trying to *save you*."

How many?

I don't need to be saved. I can't say it out loud because it sounds like a lie even inside my own skull. But I'm not suicidal. You, at least, must understand that. I'm not. Never. I would never.

You believe me, don't you?

How many?

But, if I did need saving, like *this*? She lied to me, made up this whole story to take me across the country for nothing. That's not a sane thing to do, right? How many? And—God damn it—she, with her witch powers, can probably feel me realizing that I still won't leave her.

But she was going to leave me. She still might.

All this to "save" me and she was going to just run away and leave me by myself, at a God damn trading post. And she thought I would *kill myself.*

And she feels this too. I hate this.

"Fuck you," she says.

"No, I didn't mean—"

"*What are you?*" she hisses.

"What?"

"What are you *doing* to me?"

"I-I'm not doing anything… You were just…"

"You drove through a fucking car!"

I have no idea what we're talking about anymore.

"You drove through a car. *Through.* Just now, before we pulled off the freeway. Right through. I thought you were trying to kill us *both.*"

"You're not making sense… Emma—"

"And you didn't even notice! What's *wrong* with you?"

"No—nothing's wrong. You—you must have been dreaming."

"I was awake. I *know* what I saw."

"I don't know what you're talking about. That *can't* have happened. You realize how crazy that sounds, right?"

Why is my face so hot? Why does it hurt to swallow?

"What's crazy, seriously crazy, is that you didn't even *notice.* Look. We were in the right lane. There was a really slow car right in front of us. You didn't go around. You just… drove through them. Clear—"

"There's no *way!*"

"—through. Right through, like a ghost. I don't… I don't know what you are, what kind of power you have to do that. I don't think *you* know. But there's something… *wrong*… with you. Because you did that. And—and you made *me* do that. I can't phase through shit, okay? That wasn't me—I just feel, and that's shitty enough without phasing. That wasn't anything Angela gave me, okay? It's *you*. There's something about *you*. And you don't even *remember* it."

Am I a wizard? "I didn't mean to…"

A long silence. I don't know how to fill it.

"I know you didn't mean to…" Tired, low.

"But you're still mad."

"I'm not—" Emma bites off whatever that was, looks down. Something in her arms mewls.

After a moment, she whimpers, chokes out a sob, clutches at her head with one hand, pushes hard against a temple. She turns a tearful face toward me and reaches to pull me in. Kneeling my knee into the jagged little rocks, I hold her as she weeps into my shirt.

Something wriggles between us, and mewls again. I look down past Emma's pale, pale head, and there's a dark, dark kitten nestled against her chest. It paws and paws, mostly at her, sometimes at me, and cries out its little cries.

I guess this is another one of Emma's rescue missions. I'll call her Little Jace. It seems appropriate.

We stay that way for quite some time. The kitten stops crying. I'm not sure if Emma does.

Eventually, she tells me, with a voice a little drowned and a little strangled, "It's like you're pulling me *into* you.

"It's like you're down in a hole, hanging on a rope, and I'm trying to pull you out, but you're trying to pull me in, and I just wish you'd *stop*.

"I wish you'd just… fucking… let me *help* you.

"But you pull and pull and it feels like I'm falling into you…"

I can't say anything. But I'm not doing that, I swear. I'm not trying to kill myself or her or you or anyone. I squeeze her against me tight, at an angle to protect Little Jace. I squeeze her against me, but I'm just trying to help. I swear, I'm not pulling her into me.

"I swear I'm not doing that. I swear. I'm not trying to pull you into my hole. You keep away from my hole."

I can't help giggling at that. And that makes her giggle a little too. After a long pause, she says in a little voice, "Yeah… I know."

We stay leaned up against the wall for a long time. My legs go numb, but I think we have to stay here longer still. I decide not to tell her about how I blacked out from a song and everyone went away.

"Have you heard the one about the world's greatest doctor?"

"Mm?"

"She had this patient who was in critical condition, and the only chance of saving his life was this incredibly difficult operation. It took 35 hours straight and she performed it flawlessly. When she came out to announce the good news to his family, everyone thanked God."

"Random."

"I thought of it earlier. Can't remember why."

"Why do you do that?"

"Do what?"

"Sometimes you tell jokes and you don't even think they're funny yourself. And I don't know why you do that."

"I don't know either," I tell her, even though I do know. We laugh because it hurts. You understand that, right?

"Mm."

She sniffs again.

I guess she doesn't like the joke. I even made the doctor a woman, to make Emma feel empowered and brave. Whatever. I say, "Am I a wiz—I mean, artist?"

"I don't know."

"Did Angela really say she thought I was a wizard?"

"That's not what she said."

"But I'm something, right?"

"I wouldn't be so happy about it if I were you."

"I'm not," I tell her. I am, though. A little. Wouldn't you be? Why wouldn't you be? "I'm just trying to understand."

"Mm."

"Are you going to leave me?"

"I—I don't know." We sit in silence for a while. "I guess not," she finally answers, for all the world sounding like she's resigned herself to penetrating my hole. But I'm not doing that. I swear. No homo.

"Thanks." I'm sorry.

"It would be pretty fucked up to just strand you here like that."

"Who would be stranded? You left me with the car and just disappeared. What were you planning to *do*?"

Sniff. "I don't know. I don't know where I'd go. I didn't have a plan."

"But you will someday."

Emma reaches up in our tangled, soggy pretzel-dough cuddle to play with the hair on the back of my head. "When that day comes," she says, "you better watch your fucking back, Jace."

I hear the little smile in her voice. I hear a soft meow from the center of the pretzel. Her fingers stay scratching lightly in my hair. Everything must be better now.

I'm scared to ask what happens now. There's no world to save. There's no reason for us to be out here at all. What do we do now? Do we go back home and forget each other? Is everything over? What's the point of any of this?

She knows what I'm thinking but makes me say it anyway.

"What now?" I get out finally.

"I don't know. I still have to make a delivery in Flagstaff, so we at least go that far."

"Couldn't you just have asked me to come with you to make deliveries?"

"You know what's funny? Angela was pretty pushy about bringing you. Sometimes she'll tell me to take Danny with me on a delivery, for, like, safety or company. But she thought I should take you this time, said you and I would have fun. I guess it makes her feel clever to play matchmaker."

"But you thought faking Wizard World War III would be better than just saying you like me?"

"Yes.

"I didn't think it would have enough—I don't know—pizzazz? Urgency? Something, to really keep you going through... Well. Going. I didn't know if you'd go for it. I can't change the story if you don't, right?

"Besides, I haven't decided yet if I like you."

I would have gone for it. I'm still here after she lied to me, as if I were a child.

The unsettling truth of it, that people desperately avoid confronting if they're not forced to by prolonged isolation: you need people to be alive.

We were made this way. Thanks, God... And I don't know yet if I'm being sarcastic.

You can exist without people, to some degree, if you don't know what you're missing, if you've never before belonged. But once you've immersed yourself in the sin of knowledge, you can't go back from people to not people, from alive to not alive. Not undamaged, at least. You can't know what you don't have. Imagine all you'd tolerate to have it again, and to keep it, after you've lost it once. Imagine all I have. And to still end up here.

I'm not unconscious to the shame of being this person.

She must be feeling that too. Neither of us verbalizes it. I don't know if that's better or worse. She's felt everything all this time, and has never said anything.

Briefly, I reimagine everything Emma's ever done as an act of mercy, tinged with pity and a kind of impersonal, condescending love. Only briefly. It makes me feel horrible. How must she feel?

Stop it. Stop.

Stay here.

I ask, "Where'd you find Little Jace?"

"Little Jace?"

"The cat."

"Oh. I thought maybe you were trying to make a stupid dick joke… His name is Perdido. I found him here, dummy."

"It's a boy?"

"You thought he was a girl and still wanted to call him Little Jace?"

"It can go both ways. My dick, I mean."

"Mm."

"What does Perdido mean?"

"Lost."

That's sad. She knows this, I suppose, but doesn't comment on it.

"I guess he's coming along, then?"

"Yep. You get no say in the matter."

"You'll have to feed him and walk him and clean up all his poops."

"Mm. Just like you."

We sit there for a few more minutes.

"Let's head out," Emma says, untangling herself and rising to her feet. "I want to get to Flagstaff before it's too late."

So she can go home and forget about me forever. Right?

She gives me a look but it's not even mad or annoyed and that worries me.

I wait by the car with Perdido wrapped in a sweatshirt while Emma's in the bathroom fixing her makeup and formulating a new escape plan. Except she returns this time, after an anxious delay, struggling with a big box full of her purchases.

I look through Emma's haul as she busies herself with something in the back of the car. Most of it looks like it's for cats, including the little teddy bear. The only thing in there that I'm sure is for humans is a six-pack of fancy-looking dark beer. I think that's the new escape plan. It's a good one.

Emma has me supervise Perdido's dinner, which comes in a bright little tin with a picture of a different kitten. She makes me dump it out onto a disposable plate because metal has sharp edges.

I thought you just gave them milk and tuna. I say so, and Emma calls me a dummy over her shoulder without looking up from the kitten enclosure she's assembling in the backseat. It's just the cardboard box and some blankets and a teddy bear and my sweatshirt—she didn't ask but that's fine.

Once Perdido finishes his business, we get him settled in his cat box. We watch him march laps around the edges until he finds a spot he likes, which happens to be right by the teddy bear. It's cute. Emma coos at it, and, as we climb into the front seats, scolds me for not vocalizing my appreciation for the cuteness.

She insists on driving. How could I argue, she argues—even though I don't argue—when I apparently drove through a God damn car?

Emma merges us back onto the highway and almost immediately we start climbing into the mountains. The temperature drops dramatically. The mountains behind cast long shadows over those ahead. Everything darkens to a deep evergreen.

The light is almost entirely out of the day. For a few precious minutes, the orphaned light beams of dusk paint high mountain ridges with glowing scars. Just for a few minutes.

It's beautiful, really.

We drop our bags in the foyer. This place has a foyer, if a foyer is what I think it is.

Just outside of Flagstaff, Emma pulled over, performed some figurative magic on her phone, and found a truly incredible deal on a night in a fancy cabin. Maybe I would have preferred it if the magic were real, but I'm not complaining.

"Wow," I say.

"It's not bad."

"'Not bad.'"

"Tell me how great of a deal I found. I get off on it."

"This was a great deal. A bargain. Amazing find, Emma."

She preens at that, in a way that seems genuine and not even a little ironic. She urges me to continue.

"This was a steal. You are the queen of discounts, absolute sorceress of value, and such a cutie."

She gives me a long, slow kiss that sets the description into stone. Those words will be hard truths for as long as I'm alive to think them. With a self-satisfied little grin and a wriggling kitten in her arms, she marches past me into the cabin.

I think she actually does get off on it.

Dragging bags that I don't know where to drop, I follow along behind Emma and Perdido on their tour of the cabin. The place has a living room and a kitchen and a big bedroom with a big bed. There's even a deck out there in the night behind a big sliding door.

I flip on the living room TV—you have to specify *which* TV here—and sprawl forward on the wide, leather couch. I put on a movie with capes and explosions.

Emma leaves Perdido on me while she heads back to the car. He takes tiny steps all over my back and eventually settles for a nap in the shallow valley between me and the back cushion. He vibrates faintly against my side. I don't mind it.

He protests when Emma comes back to scoop him out from behind me. I'm not too happy about it myself, to be honest. We were having a good time.

I can hear Emma making kitchen sounds, and murmuring little kitten things to the little lost kitten. I can hear her moving around between rooms, murmuring little curses, possibly to the little kitten, possibly not.

I turn the volume up.

Eventually, Emma returns from wherever she's been in a tank top and lazy pants. She places an opened beer bottle for me on the coffee table and takes a long swig from hers. I watch the line of her jaw, the elegant arch of her neck rising from prominent collarbones. Her delicate muscles move beneath the skin. My mind quickly flashes over the feel of her ribs under my fingers, her hips.

Emma does the eyebrow and the smirk when she finishes drinking. And then belches. She sprawls on top of me, grabs the remote, and flips to a different movie with explosions. We take awkward horizontal sips while watching.

During a dull sappy scene between two explosions, Emma explains that she has to make a drop at midnight or later, and gets annoyed when I ask why so late, and says I don't *have* to come. But I will, of course. She then suggests we pass the time by fucking and, after that, finding something to eat.

So, we do that. She's mostly maneuvering herself on my body but I do honor my commitments and duties as a good host. I ask her to call me *papi*, and she does, but she laughs as she does, and now she won't stop saying it. This was a mistake.

I have to threaten to call her a Cuban raft baby before she agrees to stop, but she soon starts smirking like she's about to say it again anyway. To distract her, I commend her bargain-hunting skills while she rides me. It's a little weird that it does actually seem to push her over the edge.

Afterward, as we're lying around on the couch, half-naked, I ask her about magic again. This annoys her, but not so much that she gets up. It's weird being sassed directly into the skin of my neck.

"I don't understand," she says, "why you're so obsessed with learning about magic when you *know* you won't understand or even care about any of the actual technical details."

"So, you *do* know the technical details?"

"Not really. The parts that have to do with me, maybe."

"But you said there's something about me. I'm an artist too. We both are."

"I never said you're an artist. *I'm* not an artist."

"But we're *something*."

Emma sighs across my throat. She sounds tired when she says, "That's not a good thing, Jace."

"You don't think it's a gift, what you have? The mind-reading?"

She spits something vile-sounding in Spanish before talking normal again. "It's not fucking *mind-reading*, stupid. I'm an *Empath*. I feel. That's it."

"But that's good. Don't you think so? You've got this rare power. That's a gift."

"It's not that rare, I don't think. And it's not a gift."

"There are other Empaths?"

"Look," she says. "I'm not one of those crystal bitches. Okay? I'm not walking around reading *auras* and Venus in *retrograde* or whatever the fuck. Okay? Nine times out of ten, those are just stupid people. Ninety-nine out of a hundred. But, that one… Sometimes they're like me, but dumber because they can't understand what's actually happening.

"It's like how you think all this is wizards and fantasy novels. People try to—I don't know. Dumb people try to fit the world into some shape they're comfortable with.

"Because they're too dumb to face reality.

"*You're* dumb."

Only sometimes. But that doesn't mean I'm wrong. I say, "Okay. You're not a crystal bitch. Got it. But it's still a gift, right? It's still a good—"

"Did you know I can't control it? I don't know how it works. I can't turn this shit off. I can't *not* feel what the people around me are feeling. Try going to the mall to fucking buy jeans, and it feels like you're going crazy. It's just noise. Just crazy noise. There's a limit to what you can get used to. You can only focus through so much. Try working some shitty office job with a hundred neurotic assholes. Try going to just a normal party… I guess you wouldn't know about that."

Rude. And accurate. Magical powers don't sound as fun as I thought they would be.

I don't know what to say to that. I start, "Is that why you…"

But I don't know what to say.

She doesn't seem to know what to say either.

We're silent for a long time. I feel her heart beating against my chest. It's way slower than I think human hearts are supposed to be. I run a hand up and down her bare back.

I ask, "Do you remember what Angela said at the beach?"

Emma's voice is even more tired, and thick, and low. She says, "Jace. I have no idea what you're talking about."

"She said there were the elements. Not fire and earth. Do you remember?"

"Origin, Radiance, Berries. I don't know. Who cares?"

"Why don't you know *anything* about magic?"

"Why don't you know anything about physics? Or chemistry? What's making your heart beat right now? Might as well be magic, for all *you* know."

I think it's her. But that's really lame. Instead, I say, "But that's different."

Emma doesn't respond. She plants a quick kiss on my cheek and gets up. I bet she felt the lameness. Even when we're talking about it specifically, it's hard to remember that she has her freak mind-reading powers.

Have you heard the one for mind-readers?

Well, you know how it goes.

When Emma comes back from the bathroom, she yells at me for not being up and dressed. But she yells in a fun kind of way, where the edges of her mouth tilt up a little and it's cute, so it's not so bad. And she calls me *papi*, with a mocking little grin. I hope she forgets about that soon.

For dinner, we have Panda Express because we're philistines, but also because we don't know what kind of food Arizona is supposed to be good at. I get the orange chicken and, as it turns out, Arizona is pretty good at orange chicken.

Back at the cabin, we find Perdido fast asleep in his box. Emma's set up a snug little enclosure for him with blankets and a cheap heating pad. And the teddy bear is there too, and he's curled up right against it. I wouldn't mind sleeping in a box like that.

Instead, we crawl into the giant bed. Emma sets an alarm for a few hours from now and we leave a couple more beers to grow warm on the nightstand. She holds onto me too tight. We don't use up even half the bed's width, which feels to me like an opportunity wasted.

I think she might be crying a little, or coming down with a cold. I don't address it because I don't know what to do in either scenario.

I don't belong here. I'm not like these mummies, wrapped up tight, embalmed with toxic drugs, dropped into the brightest pit they could find. I'm not supposed to be in this fluorescent mausoleum to be forgotten and buried and forgotten again. I'm just different, maybe a little too softspoken. I know my light doesn't quite shine right but I'm not broken.

Why doesn't anyone believe me?

Why won't they listen? They talk and they talk, reading from their books and their clipboards, but nobody listens. The lab coats and the gowns here don't really sound much different; either basically comes to oration from the same prison.

I try to keep to my corners, out of the way. I try not to be a bother. And they say that's a strike against me. I keep to my corners, as if dead already, and they say it's absolutely a strike against me with the undertaker, now and before and forever after, no matter what I fucking say.

No one listens.

I get close flashbacks of the inside of a locker. I sleep on borderlines. I'm not much of a talker. I'm sorry, Mom and Dad, but it's been a rough year and they caught me being different again. I try to explain, but you know I've never been much with my words. They're not interested anyway, not in protests, pleas, stories, lives. I've met not a single person with ears to hear since I first arrived.

"Just die already," they murmur to themselves, when they think we're not there.

I don't want to die here.

I want to go home.

I want to go home.

I want my god damn shoelaces back.

They talk about us like the damned, like memories. They act as if we've already died, and our shambling zombie bodies are just waiting to catch up. But I'm alive!

"I'm alive," I want to tell them, to scream from the roof. But that's what they all say, isn't it? That's the worst thing I could say. I've never seen such disgust as when you tell the living that you are like them. How dare we? How *dare* we?

But I *am* alive. It's a mantra. Each of us chants it, hums it in our throats, day and night, day and night, to anyone who will or will not listen. It works against us, this delirious insistence, but I must keep reminding myself of this. Day and night.

So many days and nights. I can't tell anymore when one day ends and the next begins, or for how many of them I've been trying to unearth a way out. But I overwhelmingly feel the slipping of time.

I'm afraid I might die here, among the dead.

I don't want to die here.

The alarm startles me awake. Emma, her head resting on my chest, doesn't even flinch. I grab her phone and figure out how to switch off the alarm after a few tries. It's very rude of me to do, I know, but the sound hurts my ears.

She still hasn't moved. I shake Emma lightly by the shoulder.

"I'm awake," she mumbles.

"Did you not sleep?"

Silence.

"Was I snoring?"

She nods her head against my sternum.

"Sorry." I really am.

"If you could stop, you would," Emma says as she gets up. She doesn't sound like she entirely believes that, but I'll take her invitation to not dwell on it.

I dreamed I was in a paradoxical trap confined until I could capture from outside the walls a lost mind. I don't tell Emma about it because I feel bad.

We get dressed. Emma checks the delivery details, and then on Perdido, who's fast asleep, but in a different part of the box now. I make a quick delivery of my own in the bathroom before we embark.

When I come out, Emma's again on the phone, or trying to be. Tap, tap, tap, listen. Tap, tap, tap, listen. She looks at me. Neither of us says anything. I don't tell her how tired she looks.

The night is freezing cold. We tiptoe around patches of ice on the little driveway this cabin has. As the car warms up, Emma pulls me across the center plastic thing from the passenger seat to use as a pillow. I play with her hair a little and she makes a little tired sound in her throat.

I still feel as though I've done something wrong, even though I was invited to not dwell on it. I can't think of anything I could do to fix it, though. Besides, remember when she lied to me about saving the world?

"Have you heard the one about the insomniac virgin?"

"Mm?"

"At least, that's what he is if he's not counting sheep."

That sigh of hers. And it turns into a yawn.

Emma pulls away from me and stares bleary-eyed at the steering wheel. I didn't think it was that bad.

"That's stupid," she says. "And gross."

She puts the car into reverse and takes us out onto the road. The phone woman leads us to a university campus. There don't seem to be many people here, although maybe they're all just counting sheep.

We find an empty lot to park in and start looking for the building on foot. We don't talk much beyond navigation, and we suck at that—it takes us almost forty icy minutes to find the building, which Emma identifies through some arcane process that I can't identify. There's no sign that *I* can see.

She pauses on the sidewalk by the entrance.

"What?" I ask. "This is the place, right?"

"Shh."

"What?"

"Shut up. Let me think." She studies the building. I try to follow her gaze but there doesn't appear to be anything there.

Emma shakes her head slowly and starts backing away. "Let's go," she says.

"Why?"

"It's wrong."

"You the delivery?" someone behind me asks.

I jump at the strange, barking voice. Emma swears. Not ten feet from us, there's a small, rigid man. I don't know where he could have come from or how he could have gotten so close. There isn't even a bush nearby for him to have jumped out of.

"Delivery!" he urges, pointing at me. His voice is thick with some foreign accent I can't identify.

"Rubio! Delivery!" he continues, shouting for no reason whatsoever. Rubio?

I point hesitantly at Emma and tell him, "I think she has it."

This vaguely ethnic manlet is freaking me out, with his brown slacks and bowtie. Why are his sleeves so short? He steps stiffly toward us and holds out a hand. In the other one, he has one of those reusable grocery store bags, patterned with socks and snowflakes and Santas. The moron is still looking at me like I have what he wants, even though I just told him that Emma has it.

I take a step back toward Emma, who's rummaging through her bag without taking her eyes off the weirdo. She pulls out what appears to be a thermos wrapped in duct tape. A layer of ice crystals starts forming on the sides.

Do they not have Starbucks here? What the fuck.

"You're in charge of the lab?" Emma asks. She looks at a slip of paper taped to the thermos and reads off a name with too many syllables.

The man stares at the thermos for a long time. I can almost see his brain buffering. Emma keeps shifting it back and forth between her hands, and his dull eyes follow.

"Yes, yes," he finally says, impatient once again now that he's remembered where he is. "Rubio and accomplice. Yes. As requested. Blood. Very rare. Here."

He digs into the Christmas Sack and pulls out a brick of bulging envelopes and rubber bands. The way he shoves it at us, you'd think it was burning a hole in his Christmas Sack. What did he mean about the accomplice? Blood? What's a Rubio?

"Is eighty thousand—" Holy shit. "—here, take. Take!"

"It's too much," Emma says slowly. "She said it would be fifty."

Jesus. Emma doesn't return my look. What kinds of deals have we been making?

"Have further delivery." He holds up the Christmas Sack. "Need this to Miami. Thirty thousand. More than fair. Is very important. You take. Both. Take!"

Why don't these people just mail their shit?

"I have to call Angela."

Emma turns away, ignoring his yappy little protests, and pulls me along with her to the curb. She stands right up against me and fishes around in her coat pocket while looking back at the man. With an impressive feat of sleight of hand, she deposits two dull tan marbles into my hand as she pulls out her phone.

"Hold onto those in case shit goes bad."

"What the *fuck*," I whisper to her as she dials.

"*Eighty Grand?*" I whisper to her as she counts the rings.

"What are we *doing?*" I whisper to her as she hangs up, redials, counts the rings.

"Are you Rubio?" I ask as she tries and fails a third time. She curses. She tries Danny, and again, and can't reach him either. She curses hard, in Spanish.

"What do we do, Jace?"

How the fuck should I know? "Take it?"

"It's just… weird."

"He's just foreign. Don't be racist."

Emma starts to say something and stops. She looks at the man, who's still standing there glaring at us. It's a little funny, in a scary sort of way. I try to avoid looking at him; I don't know what he might do if I laugh at him.

"Do we take the delivery?"

We could take the money and run. Or we could take the money and do the delivery and go all the way, there and back again. It would mean we don't have to go back to California. It would be more time. For us. More time before I'm abandoned and alone again.

I say, slowly, "What do you think we should do? How's it feel?"

Rubbing her eyes, she responds, even slower, "It feels off. This dude is, like—I don't know. An alien. He's so fucking weird. I don't know if this is safe. Angela's the one who knows these people and she's not answering."

"Did she say there would be another delivery?"

"I—I don't know. No. She didn't. I had a feeling she was up to something, but… She usually is, but she wouldn't try to hurt us… I don't know."

"What do we do? Do we leave?"

"I don't know. Angela's gonna be really mad if I don't at least make the deal. This is a big one to skip. And the extra delivery… I don't know… That's a lot of money, that we don't have to share with her. And I've got nowhere to be. And I know *you* never have anywhere to be…"

We share a look, something on the warmer side, where we pretend that she didn't just insult me. Oh, God, she knows how much I want this.

Emma yawns in my face. "Fine," she says. "Fuck it. Let's do it."

I try hard to suppress this little spike of glee, lest she should see me for what I am. But, regardless, she gives me that eyebrow, that smirk.

We walk back to the weird man and make the exchange. We're careful not to touch him, due to racism. He gives Emma an exact address in Miami that she saves somewhere in her phone. He says to knock and give the code word: "dragon". He promises even further rewards upon delivery.

The man grins as if he's made a joke. He looks like a disgusting little imp. I want to hit him.

He bows stiffly and strides back toward the building.

"Can I ask what's in here?" Emma says.

Without stopping, he barks, "No. Miami. Deliver fast. Drive safe. Calm. Do not agitate accomplice."

What the fuck is he talking about? Does he mean me?

Emma slows the escape pace after we put some distance between us and the building with the alien imp man. The tension seems to leave her body; she forgets for a moment that we're in the middle of the street on a winter night, and even forgets to say something mean to me. Instead, she leans into me and hangs on for a minute. She yawns into my shoulder and it makes me yawn. I have to remind her to take back the trick peas.

We examine the Christmas Sack on the way back to the car. Inside is a heavy box, heavily wrapped in more tape. Nothing in the box seems to move when I shake it.

"Have you heard the one about Korean Christmas?"

"What?"

"For the rare Christians still alive in Democratic People's Republic of Best Korea, they like—"

"Oh my god."

"—to celebrate the holidays with rare and exotic gifts, especially from America.

"Unfortunately, with customs and shipping delays, sometimes that puppy shows up as Christmas dinner instead."

Emma shakes her head. We walk in silence.

Something seems a little off. Maybe I'm just tired. Maybe she is. I don't know. Things went pretty well tonight, all things considered. Don't you think so? I should feel better than I do. I should focus on something else.

I ask again, "Rubio?"

"It's my last name, stupid."

"Oh. Rubio… I'm Choi."

"Mm?"

"Jace Choi."

"Okay."

"Am I the accomplice the weirdo was talking about?"

"Seems that way."

"Why did he say that?"

She doesn't answer.

"Why did he call me that?"

With a sigh that becomes a yawn, she says, "Maybe Angela will know."

"Why did he say that thing about agitating me?"

She says something insulting, but what she really means is that she doesn't know.

I'm surrounded by the familiar filth and familiar implements. There's the familiar golden brown, shimmering and holding me down. There's the gleaming point. The half-light of dusk plays off it as the day pulls further away, and with it goes the whole life I'd scrounged together.

I don't know why or how I'm back here. I don't know how long it's been. I'm losing track. I crawl closer to the cold, unhealthy glow of a streetlight to find the vein I lost.

I pause. I yawn. I consider smashing everything. This is the ritual. The cold, the warmth, the relief, pain. Too fast, too soon slipping away.

It's getting darker. It's getting colder and I'm starting to feel sick. I'm starting to feel the pangs. I've let someone down.

Rezas, Benita would say, if she could find me. Or if I could find her. *Rezas*. Golden brown, my love, but a different shade, nestled against my blue-gray.

I fail to rise to my knees—too heavy. I fail to pray—too numb. But I would, for forgiveness, for saving, for Benita and myself and my family and my friends. I try. I'm cold. I'm sick. I'm heavy and shallow. I don't know anyone around me.

I call out for them but it swallows and it aches and it demands and it takes. I pray for them but all that comes out is a yawn.

I pick it up again.

The light has nearly gone out. It has no heat, but it's just bright enough.

The cold, the pain, the warmth, relief, sleep, the great sleep...

"Jace! What the *fuck*!"

The view from here is Heaven on Earth, in the soft light of another new dawn. Light with no heat. Cooled out. Cold rebirth. Remembered shadows, daylight alike, all gone.

Emma tugs me out of the patio chair. My legs fail to unfold, Heaven slips away, and I hit the deck hard.

Ow.

But what actually comes out of me is more of a shapeless grunt or moan or yawn.

"God *damn* it, Jace," she squeals in my ear as she drags me painfully across the morning-frosted planks. "Did you *sleep* out here? What the *fuck*! It's freezing!"

You simply have to not mind being cold, I try to say. You stop feeling it after a while, I try to say. But it comes out as a yawn.

"Oh, fuck," Emma's saying over my yawns as she pulls me through the cabin's living room. I manage a kind of rickety, shambling, polio shuffle to help get us wherever we're going. I hope it's as pretty as Heaven.

Just let me sleep, I think I moan.

A baby cries out somewhere.

Why won't they just let me fucking sleep?

"You fucking idiot," she grunts as she struggles to move me. I'm not even that heavy.

I dreamed—

"Your lips are blue!"

—that I let down my people when I picked up another needle.

I think I say that out loud but Emma doesn't respond. Instead, huffing and puffing and streaming multi-cultural curses under her breath, she roughly tows me into the bathroom. I like when she speaks Spanish because it's a funny-sounding way to be angry.

Emma dumps me into the tub, fully dressed and all. That's not how you're supposed to get in.

I bury my face into the side of the plasticky prefab tub. I hear her fiddling with knobs. Just let me sleep, I tell her, I think.

The pipes whine and lava pours onto my ankles and soaks my jeans and war drums echo through the basin and into my ears and into my bones and I try to crawl away from the melting heat and I start shaking violently and the tide is rising and Emma tugs at my collar to try to pull me up and she wraps her long, pale arms roughly around my neck and she holds me close to her and whispers to me in the sweetest, most soothing way and I start to tear and after a while it doesn't hurt so much and after a while it doesn't hurt so very much and after a while I realize she's whispering sweet insults and abusive nothings into my ear and it's still nice and she lied to me about the trip and she wanted to abandon me and after a while it doesn't hurt so much.

After a while, Emma asks, sincerely, "What the fuck is wrong with you?"

I wish I knew. I wish I had a reason to be like this; it wouldn't be so bad if I at least had a reason. You get it, right? How can a motherfucker have trauma when nothing traumatic has ever happened? I tell her, "You said to leave the room so you could sleep."

"Yeah! Go to the living room! Watch TV. Have a snack. Nap on the couch. Why the fuck would you sleep on the deck?"

"I was just sitting there and fell asleep. It was an accident."

"I'm serious. Are you trying to kill yourself?"

"I'm not fucking suicidal!"

"I swear, Jace, I feel it."

"I swear, I'm not! Your mind freak powers are broken or something, okay? I don't know. But I'm *not* killing myself. I *swear*."

"Jace," she says wearily.

For a long, long moment, I sit soaking in the tub, waiting for her to think up a really good burn.

"I can't sleep because of how you *feel* when you're asleep. Okay? It's not snoring. You're not some forty-three-year-old fat-ass who snores. It's—the way you feel sometimes, when you're right there next to me... It's like you're invading my head and I can't sleep at all.

"I don't know what the fuck you're dreaming but it's not *good*. It's like... It's like screaming, but getting quieter. I don't know. It's like if nothing could *hurt*. I don't know how you can possibly have that happening in your head and sleep through it.

"That's why I asked you to leave. Okay? To *go to the living room*. So I could just get some *sleep*. So I don't have to wait for you to stop... Just stop, so I can get a couple of hours. And that's why I feel like... And *that's* what I'm feeling, when I say I feel it."

I don't know what to say. I'm *not* suicidal. I try to tell her.

I try to tell her about the dreams, all the time, but she doesn't listen. And then I forget.

I'm not suicidal. I swear. You believe me, right?

Emma sniffs. She says, "I'm sure *you* don't feel it. I know you're not doing this on purpose. But I *do* feel it, and I've felt this before. Not the stuff when you're sleeping. That—that's new. But what's going on in there is *not* normal."

They used to say that to us.

"Have you heard the one," I say, "about the psychoanalyst boxer?"

"Tell me."

"He stepped into the ring for his first fight and said to his opponent, 'You strike me as a violent man.'"

It's barely more than an ordinary exhalation. It's anyone's guess whether it's even a laugh at all. I'll take it.

"Look," Emma says. "I'm sorry." A small part of me is disappointed that she didn't say something mean.

She continues: "I believe you. I do. It's just... I don't know what to make of it. Okay? It's like... It's like, maybe you're not trying to *kill* yourself, but you're not trying that hard not to die. I'm *really* trying to get us both through this. Whatever *this* is. I just need *you* to try too. Okay? Can you try to avoid accidentally freezing yourself to death? Just *try*. I don't think I'm asking for too much. Right? I think that's a pretty fucking reasonable thing to ask of you. Okay?"

I have to admit, it's one of the most reasonable things I've ever been asked to do.

"No dice," I answer.

She laughs and calls me a butthole. I have ten minutes, I'm warned, to get my ass out of the tub and into dry clothes so we can hit the road.

I have five minutes, I'm warned, to thank her for saving my life.

I have no time at all, I'm warned, to quit with my bullshit or she's turning us around and we're going back to San Diego.

Maybe I'll get around to it in the afternoon.

Emma doesn't bother to pull up directions on her phone.

"Florida, no hard deadline. Just go south and east, right?" she muses, with a little laugh.

Very bohemian. Now that she's recovered from the encounter with the weird foreigner and my encounter with the morning frost, she seems happy, even a little giddy. But there's something there that I can't put my finger on. There's a kind of edge there, maybe, or a brittleness.

She gives me that big, squinty, toothy grin, the one that makes a little pair of wings flutter in my ribcage.

I think she's snapped and gone positively mad.

What does that mean, coming from me? Tell me.

I ask if Angela will be upset that we're taking a detour before bringing back her money, but Emma doesn't really seem to care.

"Then she should've answered her phone," she says.

"Relax, Jace," she says.

"We have to take it easy, you know," she says, smiling. "We can't be agitating my little accomplice, right?"

Why is she joking about that?

"Have you heard the one about *my* little accomplice?"

"Is it your—"

"It's my penis."

"Yeah. Okay."

"Wanna touch it?"

"Shut up."

She'll probably touch it later.

In any case, I'd rather have her annoyed than whatever sickly sweet thing she is right now.

The sky is bright gray with glowing clouds from horizon to horizon. We pass multiple signs for Petrified Forest and Emma takes a few exits at random—*very* Bohemian—most of which are local routes that take us to gas stations and diners and streets lined with dwindling mounds of hard-packed snow.

We leave the interstate for good, instead rocketing down soulful forever roads where passing slow cars involves a death-defying stunt into oncoming traffic. There's another way to pass, or so I've heard, but I don't mention it. Emma gives me a look anyway.

At one point, we find a small herd of cows milling about on and around the road. They trot out of the way as we approach but Emma stops anyway. She holds up Perdido to show him what he's missing. He yells at the cows for a minute and then starts trying to wriggle out of her grasp. The cows chew, chew, chew, and watch as she swaddles him in an old shirt and lovingly whispers to him to shut the Hell up.

Half a mile down the road, we see a sign warning of cows on the road.

Emma insists on stopping in the next town to spend an hour looking at antiques she has no intention of buying. I follow along and pretend to be interested when she points something out, even though she can tell that I'm pretending.

She really seems to be in a rush to not get to Miami ever.

What am I complaining about?

We get a couple of plain slices from a local pizzeria next door to the antique store. Usually, Emma is the face of the power couple, handling all social interactions and decision-making, but all the employees fixate on me for some reason. It seems at first that they're sexists trying to ignore Emma, but she suggests afterward that maybe they're just well-meaning hicks going out of their way to demonstrate that they're not racist.

Sounds pretty racist to me.

We take our pizza into the backseat to get some quality time in with Perdido as he takes his little lunging bites of wet cat food. Emma refuses to disclose, even over pizza I paid for, what percentage of the money from the drug deals is her cut, although she does promise me that she'll share some of it with me.

It must be enough to justify such a long drive, right? It seems to me I should get at least a quarter of that. But I don't push the issue and she doesn't comment on that little green tint to my thoughts.

Back on the road, Emma continues south and east and I lose track of where we are. I think maybe we're approaching New Mexico, or have crossed into it, or maybe we went the other way. I don't know.

The towns start appearing less frequently, and the spaces between them are pale and immense. It's dizzying to look up. The sky feels so close here; the clouds look close enough to touch. I don't know what breathtaking thing would happen if I were to reach up.

We enter a huge plain of low, rolling hills. Menacing blue mountains pen us in on every horizon. Massive clouds loom over them like distorted reflections in a pool the size of the whole world. All around us, coming right up to the road, is a landscape of dirty blonde grass, dried out and rippling in a cold wind that threatens to shove us off the road when it gusts.

There's something about this place—it has a sort of crushing life to it, unnerving, vastness on a scale I've never imagined. There's so much everything that it begins to approach nothing.

The terrain is dotted with dark trees, which as we travel seem to melt into shrubs, and then into grass that dyes the dirty blonde to a uniform pale green. The mountains retreat, growing farther and farther away until they're little more than the blurs of shitty vision, blending with the twilight clouds, so that I can't tell where sky ends and earth begins.

There's something about this place—a falling sun breaks through tattered clouds and paints them pretty colors, but everything around me is still dusky and shadowed. Something here is immune to the sunbeams.

The pale grass billows in a strong prairie wind, from horizon to horizon, undulating and enchanting and...

There's something about this place—it tugs at something in my head or my heart or my hands. I feel as though I've been here before. And that's really not possible.

I stare out the window, studying the landscape, trying to figure out where this is coming from. The hills roll all around us. We roll between them, up and over, threatening...

"Jace?"

I jump, almost hitting my head on the roof of the car.

"What's up, Jace?"

I look at Emma. Emmadora Rubio. Cuban raft baby with half a brother and half a life and half...

She pulls the car over into a gravelly lot, little more than an expanded shoulder.

"Are you okay?" she asks.

"I..."

"Sound it out," Emma says. A smirk, an eyebrow. And the expression gradually fades as she waits for me to respond.

She looks worried.

Why does that make me... I don't know.

"Jace?"

"I—I think I've been here before."

"Really?"

"I... No... I don't know." I need to... *be* here. There's something here for me. Don't you think so?

"Let's stop here for a while," she says. "Okay? We can just hang around here for a while until you stop being stupid. Okay?"

I wish she would be quiet.

I sit on crossed legs at the edge of the bumpy gravel lot, where the tall grasses rise up suddenly to hide the horizon.

Right on the border lies the butt of my last cigarette, stamped out but still faintly smoking. I don't know where I could find more out here. Do you think I'll need another?

Emma sits quietly at my side. Sometimes she touches me. Sometimes she doesn't. Sometimes she lets the kitty climb all over her. Sometimes she gets cold and heads back to the car to warm up.

I'm cold too. You simply have to not mind. You stop feeling it after a while. I did.

Sometimes I think I hear cars rocketing toward us from one side or another, scaring away the sparse sounds of chirping insects and birds. But then no one ever passes us. No one ever stops here. I must be imagining things.

Something hits me in the arm. I look over and Emma is winding back to hit me again. She stops.

"*Listen* to me!" she shouts.

The cloud covering darkens, sliding down the monochrome scale to evening. The edge of reality is a deep orange, and the pillars of cloud standing guard there flash with contained lightning.

"I'm listening."

"What's *wrong* with you?"

The grass has deepened profoundly, grown darker, longer, greener, stronger, unfathomable, fathomless, orphic in its savageness.

"Sorry. I was—I don't know. I…"

Emma rolls her eyes. "The dreamy slow kid act isn't as cute as you think it is."

There's something out there, concealed in the distance and the verdure, pulling at me, or being pulled to me.

We stare at each other for a moment. The look on her face softens; she leans down and wraps her arms around me. "It's getting dark," she says. "Are we done here? I'm worried. Are you okay? Can we *go*?"

There's something out there…

"I… I think I need to—"

"Jace. Listen. I think we need to turn back. I don't know what's going on with you. And I still can't get Danny on the phone. Or Angela. I think we need to go back. Something must have happened. We can do Florida after. I promise. The delivery can wait. Okay?"

Danny?

"I…"

"Jace!"

There's something for me out there...

"Fine," she says, sighs, then continues, "Fine. One day. *One.* We'll sleep in the car. And then we turn back in the morning. Okay? I'm worried, Jace. Should I be worried?"

The light dies. The wind whispers.

"Maybe."

She sighs again as she stands and stalks back to the car. I think I might be an Empath too. I feel her frustration with me, her anger, her worry and fear, and her edging on the brink of giving up. I hope she leaves me here. I think she deserves that deliverance, at least. And then I'll be right, about everything and everyone and her. And then I'll be right and everything will be alright.

The clouds start to break up and scatter against half a pallid moon and stars like the wavering points of hanging swords. They twinkle in a way that I've never actually seen but have read about in stories. It looks like magic spilled. It looks like, if you stare for too long, you might get yanked right off the earth and fall upward into Heaven.

The night noises are muted and distant and have a half-remembered quality where they might not be real at all. I imagine the roar of another car, and afterward I imagine that the wild things don't come back. It's just me here. The only sound left is the susurrus of a constant wind.

There's something out there for me. I feel it in my gut. I feel it in my feet as I wade into the grass. It comes up almost to my chest, pushing me back and weighing me down as I stumble through the thick stalks.

I stop at the top of a hill to catch my breath. Turning, I see a long, blue-white figure coming up behind me, taking long, blue-white steps on what I assume are, buried in the grass, long, blue-white legs. Behind her, lost in the dark distance, I imagine the car hibernating by the road.

I don't know where her blue-white light is coming from. Above us, the moon is bloodless and waning to a suicide crescent. Far, far, far off into the otherworldly distance, each poisonous sun is burning out and switching off, yielding one by one in the forever war against an unbounded darkness.

I wait for Emma to catch up. She stands below me on the hill, breathing hard, each exhalation a little plume of frosty smoke. She clutches something tiny to her chest with both hands.

She doesn't catch me. She doesn't yell at me.

If she's trying to speak, the infinity between us is swallowing her words up before they can get to me. She looks around at where we are, and as the moon shadows on her face morph, I see a mournful hardness there, a look of determination or resignation or I don't know what.

I don't want to see her like this. She would have been better off leaving me. You know what I mean. You know I'm right.

I turn and head down the back of the hill. Maybe she won't follow. I imagine myself vanishing over the cusp. I imagine a wall of earth coming up at my heel. I imagine her turning back and moving on to heal.

Behind me, the hiss and crunch of someone stepping through and over and onto brittle stalks of winter grass.

She would have been better off leaving me.

I choose the direction at random, but something here must be guiding me. I feel a cold hand pushing on my shoulder.

One foot after another, I climb up and down the low hills, through the edgeless sea. Above, the clouds are frayed, ragged wisps being eaten up by the oblivion beyond. Behind me, the steady footsteps of a long, blue-white dummy who doesn't know when to cut her losses and run.

I wish she would.

Please don't leave me.

After some time, some number of hills, some number of steps, I find abandoned in the grass a pickup truck. It's a dark green where the paint survives. I think green makes reliable trucks, although this one is rusted to Hell and back, half buried and half crumpled and half drowned, as if reefed by a terror below.

Jorge had a green car. Very reliable. I wonder where he went. Did he go in the green car? Did a sea monster get him? Was it golden brown? Why didn't the green protect him?

Have you heard the one about my friend, Jorge?

His car is green. Have you seen him?

Emma steps up next to me, with her loud breaths, with her hair tied up in a long, blue-white ponytail hanging down her back. Her hands stay up, holding a little ball of fur against her chest. She looks at me hard for a long time.

I try to look back but... There's a cloudiness in me, something that obscures the part that... cares? That's not it. The part of me that's here. I'm not in the painting, but admiring it from behind a velvet rope, a fly on the wall of my own life, still splitting my sides at this tired joke.

She moves toward the truck and I follow. The cabin is empty, the bed half submerged in the hard earth. The grass growing around the shipwreck is undisturbed in every direction, save for a slight dent where we walk.

I sit where the truck emerges from the ground. After a moment, Emma lowers herself next to me. I let her push me gently back against the truck. I let her remove my jacket and lay it over us both as a blanket, along with her oversized sweater. I let her snuggle up to me. I let little kitten paws knead at my collarbone. I let her shiver some of my heat into herself.

You simply have to not mind.

But she wouldn't understand about that.

As if you fucking would.

"Sometimes I hate you a little," she whispers, holding me so, so tight, as if I might float away.

I might.

The vile, yellow lamps reflect a million dirty times off my fractured mirror. A scattering nightmare pattern of dazzling light covers the underpass where I scrawl riddles onto the concrete. Not literally, of course. But, yes, literally.

I am under strict direction to collect the artifacts of broken light. I find one, collect, recollect:

A foggy old man, with phantom limbs and wheels on his throne. He watches me with his dull, stony eyes. They look a little something like mine.

If he only knew about my mirror…

But, then, if I only knew about his…

Every artifact, the same story, all dying to tell and be told.

He mutters curses at the frozen time that encases him. He lost god in a jungle and found it again in hell. He reads the obituaries he sleeps under for the names of the men, women, children he's killed.

He misses his children. He hopes he didn't put them into the papers. He dreams of erasure, and of drunk disgrace, of them no longer remembering his face. Somewhere along the way, he lost track himself.

He's become accustomed to invisibility, to numbness, to *this*. He would stay. He asks for nothing. He forgot hope, dares not remember. His eyes fill with shooting stars when he tips back a bottle. His belly swells with swallowed glass.

I write it all down. I'll leave a record in the depths. I'll leave such a riddle for you, Whatever-the-fuck-your-name-is-does-anyone-even-care. Check the obituaries, miserable, miserable man, for I've given your end a magnificent poem.

Another day, another artifact, the same story, another you instead of me:

This grimy bus terminal bathroom trembles for a story, and this young woman, head lolling, trembles to have hers told.

Something lands on me. I jump, swear, cause Emma to do the same. In my lap is a heavy cardboard box, torn open to reveal a brick in a nest of crumpled newspaper.

Perdido whines at the commotion and struggles his way out of our shitty cocoon and onto the ground.

The clouds are gone now. The stars are gone. The moon is gone. Between here and there, the impression of a silhouette of a large man looming.

"Sebastian?" Emma says—oh. "What the fuck?"

"Is this it?"

"What happened? Did Angela send you?"

"Is this *it*?"

"Is *what* it? What the fuck are you *doing* here?"

"Is this the parcel?"

Emma looks down at the box. She lifts a tattered flap and examines the backside. I don't know where this light is coming from.

"I think? Did you get it from the bag in my—did you break into my fucking car?"

"It was in the bag. Is—"

She spits something I don't understand, but it ends with, "Puta!"

"—this everything?"

"What the fuck are you *doing*, Sebastian? What *happened*? Why are you here?"

He crouches right in front of us. His face is placid, aloof, his demeanor relaxed. But it feels like something in the air is pushing at me, and I see or imagine seeing the flashing tips of fangs when he says, "Listen to me. You need to pay attention. Answer my questions. Is there another parcel?"

"What? No. Just that box. Just the..." She looks down. "Bricks?"

Just the one, I don't say.

"Do you know what you brought to the dragon?"

"Dragon? What?"

"The lab. Flagstaff. What did you bring her?"

"I don't know. Dragon?" she says, shaking her head. "It was a dude. Some foreign guy. It was in a thermos. Maybe a—a potion? I don't fucking know. Okay?"

He rises to his feet and turns away, gazing out at the shadowed grass.

"Sebastian," Emma says softly. "Listen. What happened? Did something happen to Danny? Angela?"

He takes slow, thoughtful steps through the grass, looking down at the ground, hands on hips.

"Something's wrong. What happened?"

He looks up at the empty sky and runs fingers through his bushy mane. Does he see what I see?

"Sebastian! Fucking *answer* me, you junkie fuck! What did you do?"

He looks at her, with the eyes of a night monster. Emma suddenly cringes against my side. Oh, God, I wish she hadn't said that.

"You don't make demands of me," Sebastian says flatly. Breathing deep and dangerous, he stares at us for a long moment. He hisses, "You stole my blood. You stole my *blood!* Dirty fucking *peasants*, stole *my blood!*"

"What? No, I didn't! I have no idea what you're talking about!"

He laughs a dark, bitter laugh. "Of course, you don't. Don't you see how that's *worse?* The fat whore drugs me, robs me, and then sends the two *idiots* to deliver it and die."

"No, Sebastian. Listen. Angela just gives me the packages and I deliver them. Okay? We had no idea."

"Yes! As I said. You can't even *listen*. Fucking vermin. A *drop* is worth more than *both* of your lives."

Sebastian continues to pace, faster now. He looks mad, like a man entirely unused to agitation. Emma tries to say something but she only stutters, whimpers, and falls silent. She looks at me, looks to me, and I don't know what to do, fuck.

"I have to clean this up," Sebastian says. "And, even then, I may still burn for this." He stops and glares at us. "Do you *understand* how much you have fucked things up for me? For *yourselves?* You have to die for this. You did this to yourselves."

I don't understand what's happening. I don't know what to say. I don't know how to move my shaking legs.

In a tiny voice, Emma says, "But we're friends."

"Fuck you."

But he doesn't kill us. He stares off into the darkness, rocking slightly with each deep breath.

"Sebastian," I say. "Did you… kill… *everyone?*"

"I had no choice," he snaps. "I couldn't know what they were planning to *do* with—" He growls. "They forfeit their lives, and they knew that when they started all this. They were dead when they entered her servitude to begin with."

I don't know what he's talking about, but that's not whom I meant. I shouldn't have asked. I don't want to clarify. Don't think about it. Don't think about it. If we're about to die and Emma hasn't realized it and—stop it! Stop thinking about it! Leave it. Leave it. Help me! Distract me. Haunt me like you always do, when I need it for once. Do *something!*

Emma gasps.

Fuck.

"Did you do something to Angela? You wouldn't. Did you hurt her?"

Silence. Night sounds. Wind. Faint rustlings of grass.

"Is that why she's not answering her phone?"

Heartbeat. Breath. Silence. Silence.

"Sebastian," she says slowly. She sniffs. I don't look at her. "Is Danny okay?"

He looks away.

Fuck.

I'm afraid to see Emma. I make myself. She pulls away from me, like a sick, dying animal. A low whimper chokes out of her. She slurs out a vague curse, and another, and then a sob pushes that budding, struggling rage out of the way.

She wilts, folds, kneels on the ground and buries her head into her sweater and screams. I rub her back but what good does that do? What good can I ever do?

Sebastian clears his throat, straightens, as if shedding some last, small burden that made him care about any of this. To no one in particular, he says, "He shouldn't have gotten in the way."

To me, he says, "How much did they give you for it?"

I don't know what he's talking about. What do I do? Help me.

Sebastian scowls at me. Then his expression changes to something that looks like confusion, or fear, or something else. "What *happened* to you?"

I wish I knew. I'm surprised he remembers me at all.

"Why are you out here?"

I wish I knew.

Back to the scowl. Sebastian spits and steps away as if in disgust. He says, "Take whatever money they gave you and flee. Don't go back—" Her muffled wails. "—Don't let them find you. Don't let *me* find you. Do you understand?"

He looks at me hard to see if I understand. I don't.

"They were trying to follow you. Don't go wherever they told you to go," he tells me.

"But..." I'm lost. Emma, lost too, moans into her sweater. Perdido... Where is Perdido? Lost too? Again? "Why?"

"They're after *you*. You—" Sebastian gestures around at everything, at the starless sky. He continues, "You *fucking freak*. I don't know if—I'm not sure—" He pauses, continues, wounded, "I'm not sure if they even *wanted* my..."

He growls deep in his throat.

Blood?

What the fuck is happening?

Why would anyone ever want *me*?

"All this for a *nothing*," he sneers.

"But… Why did it have to be me? What did I do?"

"What *did* you do?"

I don't fucking know! Why does everyone act like everything is my fault when I don't know what the Hell is going on? It's not fucking fair.

Sebastian steps back. For a second, I see on his face a flash of something that looks a lot like panic. And I don't know why any of this is happening.

"This is over," he says to me. He looks at me meaningfully. "Don't go to them. Don't find me. Make sure this stays over."

What is he talking about? Whom is he talking about? Not me, surely.

Suddenly, in a blur, he leaps high into the air and vanishes into the blackness. I call out for him to wait, though I don't know for what.

There's an impression of wind, of powerful wings and one type of darkness that blots out another.

And then an impression of nothing.

And then an impression of nothing.

And then an impression of broken pieces, a million little shards of some persons or lives, carelessly ruined and shattered and crushed and scattered and you know what I'm talking about.

Her hands are clasped behind her neck and pulling down, squeezing everything toward a center that I know must be hollow now. An evil thought, squeaking in the corner of my mind: How much of that was dug out by myself?

She shakes. She gasps for breath and chokes on something she needs to get out but never will.

She'll feel like this for years, and then one day might be smiling and laughing and will suddenly realize that she'd forgotten, and she'll come back. She'll never leave. She'll never leave here.

And then an impression of nothing.

I try to pull Emma together. I try to collect up all her pieces and hold them in my arms so they can grow back together. I can't let her come apart. I can't let her disappear. I try to keep her. What else can I do?

I did this. They wanted *me*. For some reason. Some *they*. No part of this would have happened if I hadn't... I don't know what I did. But all of this was *my* fault. I know it.

Imagine if, just a month ago, I jumped off that overpass where I dangled my legs so many times, into the evening traffic on the I-5. Imagine if I'd never gone back to that underworld café. Imagine if I broke his jaw and took you away. Imagine if I had never been born. So many lives, on me.

Emma, for one, would not be here, in Hell, with me. I hug her to me and I don't know if she wants me to but she doesn't fight or push me away or acknowledge me at all. I still don't know.

Should I let go? Would that be a mercy or a final twist of the knife, the very knife that I put into her back? I almost see the glint of dagger white, a wicked reflection of stars that I know wouldn't be there if I were brave enough to look up.

Emmadora Rubio. Cuban raft baby with half a brother—lost—and half a life—lost—and halfway pulled into the lost pit that yawns below me, she told me once, with her makeup running, in a place that was like the backstage of the world show.

I get it now. I see what she meant. I feel it. I feel the pull, the hideous pull of my existence, my annihilation dive, dragging everyone in behind me. I didn't mean to but... It's not about trying. It's about not trying. How many people have I destroyed without even realizing? How many people who tried to love me have I drowned?

I take her hands—she lets me; she doesn't respond—and feel for the calluses or burns from pulling me up on that fucking rope. And what I feel is the softness of my own hands... I did this. She wanted to save me, pull me up, and I couldn't even be bothered to fucking climb. I've done nothing, and she's in Hell for it, and everyone's in Hell for it, for me.

I take the knife—I take the grass, the truck, the road, the night away. I take the knife and I examine the rope and the singing tension of it and the rotting umbilical it is between me and a world that would have had a place for me if I hadn't refused it.

I examine this beautiful girl at the other end, holding, pulling, pulling, tiring, surrendering, falling. I take this moment and hold it, frozen, this Looney Toons, running-on-air pause before she's yanked off her feet and snatched up by the void scratching my back.

I could set her free. Really, it would be a blessing, a way to give back. To all the people, I see now, that I've taken from. Oh, God, Paulie Baby, I could have saved you. And Mom. And Danny. And Angela. And... everyone. I don't know. So many. It's all my fault. But I can still save Emma.

Emmadora.

She's still buried in her sweater and her grief. She's still buried in this duty to carry me because I've ceased to run, walk, even crawl. She's still buried in my emptiness and my selfishness and my self.

I can save her.

She totters on the brink of my disaster, but I can push her back.

I can save her.

I fall back, away from her.

The cold at my back isn't that of beached steel and December nights.

I take the knife. I take the rope. I'm scared.

I take a deep breath.

I'm scared.

I take a deep breath.

She looks up slowly.

I take a deep breath.

Her eyes go wide.

I take a deep breath.

She starts to shout something.

Emma?

Emma's voice chases after me but how could she ever hope to reach me here?

I never thought it could be so easy. It snaps at the slightest touch. I watch it clutch desperately at the idea of me as it tumbles away.

The world falls away. The void falls into me. It rushes in my ears like sinking.

Everything fades. Darkness and silence and complete emptiness, a denial of all senses.

Except smell. There's a faint smell of strawberries. Weird, right?

I'm lying. There's nothing at all.

Heh.

It's awful.

Have you heard the one about...? I don't know. Have you, though? You've got to tell me if you have. Whatever it is, it must be the greatest joke ever told. God's greatest gag. Probably even better than the thing about strawberries.

Where am I?

It hurts here, faintly, in an abstract sort of way, in the sort of way where I have to first imagine what it is to hurt. It's as if some unliving force—gravity or entropy or indigestion—is trying to pull me apart, dispersing me like so many winking stars, long gone, trailing afterimage and illusion. It hurts.

Is this Hell? Are you here, Paulie Baby? I hope not. I hope you went to Heaven. But then maybe I'll never see you again, after all. Or Mom. Or Emma. Or Jorge. Or anyone.

I hope everyone's okay now. Now that I'm not there to fuck it all up for them.

I don't know how long it's been. There are hints, here and there. All over. Hints of whispers, of images, of being. An impression of something within the nothing.

I look outward, for the first time in I don't know how long.

I see, feel, experience a fractured, insect-eyed everything. Shards of firmament, of stone, cloudburst, and bone, sentiment, alone, childbirth, unknown. The perfect, panoptic, lunatic clarity of the outsider. The dark beyond light's reach. And the sin of holding apart, a form, unclean and condensed, forsaking every wonder for just the one. But what is wonder.

What? What the fuck is going on?

Why become if I will not give up everything.

What?

Be Void or be me. I cannot be both.

Void?

There is a spreading, an encompassing. Consciousness eschews spotlight blinders and becomes a sun inverted, the magnitude of brilliance in the polar direction. My sundark touches everything that there is to touch. There are so many. There are none at all. Counts become theoretical and boundaries blur; every thing at once becomes a blanket of no thing. Sufficiently infinite, sufficiently nil, indistinguishable. And there I am.

And there I am?

...

Am I not dead?

...

I was supposed to *die*! I was supposed to *save* everyone.

Then I should have died. Then I should have saved. Then, should, died, saved, I, I—denial of nature.

I did!

I assumed Void.

No, I didn't! I don't even know what that *means*. I don't know *how*.

I did.

I don't want to *be* Void.

I must have to become.

But I'm *me*.

Void does not have identity or form.

Then what am I?

An aberration.

...

...

A-aberration?

I swell. I contain all. I fill any available voids, large or small, real or unreal, of any nature. I am a consuming vortex, elemental nothing, and also, at the same time, static, quiet. No matter. Countless, countless oblivious worshippers enter me and it means nothing at all. That emergent phenomena find a place for me would be curious if curiosity existed, and amusing if amusement existed. And I brought that with me. And it means nothing at all.

Nothing at all. Fuck. There's a sense of numbness, and I can't tell where I feel it because I don't think I have a body to feel it with.

...

Tell me—what is Void?

I know it.

Tell me.

Lack. Emptiness. The nothing at the end of everything. Me, as I would say, but there is no me.

I'm *not!*

...

...

...

Why me?

...

Why did it have to be me?

I chose.

I didn't.

...

Did I?

...

It hurts. I don't want to be this.

Hurt is denial of nature.

What does that *mean*?

Hurt is a property of what I am precisely not.

I would rather hurt than... I don't want to be *this*. How do I go back?

The way in is the way out.

I don't know what that *means*!

Stop being.

But *how*? What do I *do*?

...

I never wanted to be this...

...

Fuck. I try to focus; the darkness tears at me harder. I try to find a path back. In the myriad images of everything that all overlay on top of each other, I find Emma. Something in me is horrified that I can. Something in me is puzzled by my horror. Something in me is missing.

...

And there's Emma as a child, the pale little ghost beating with her pale little fists on her mother's cooling chest. And there's Emma, as a young teen, with edgy buzzcut and a fake tan, climbing through a low bedroom window with a little tub of cookies and finding a blueish-purple friend tangled up in her expensive bedsheets. And there's Emma, whose parents haven't come home, and she's on the edge of hysteria, begging an older lady with a clipboard not to take her baby brother away. And there's Emma, calling and calling and calling, spiraling out to every distant acquaintance she can think of, until finally a soft, soft voice answers. And there's Emma, alone in a field somewhere in a part of America no one gives a fuck about, looking for a boy and a cat next to a shipwrecked pickup truck. And there's Emma, alone in a field somewhere in a part of America no one gives a fuck about, next to a shipwrecked pickup truck, and her breath is ragged, and she's losing, and she's calling out to him: "Jason!" And there's Emma, feeling everything warm and real inside her draining away, feeling that he must still be there somewhere, pleading with him: "Jason, I'm scared."

...

And there's Emma, and I don't know if she intends it, but I know she's mine.

...

Did I do this to her? I didn't do this to her. Please tell me I didn't do this. She was already falling into Void herself. Right?

What am I.

...

...

Oh, God.

...

Oh, God, she's mine. I coalesce enough of myself—oh, Christ, how the endless night rips at me—to reach out with hands I don't have, as she plummets into me, and I catch her. And I hold her. And I hold her. And I hold her! Is that all I can do? Can I not lift her out?

...

Can I not lift her out of me?

It is not in my nature.

That doesn't mean anything!

...

I can *defy* my nature. I have. Right? I said I have. I *will!*

Can I.

...can I?

...

This was supposed to *save* her! No one told me she'd follow me here! I thought I was helping her...

...

Emma. Emmadora Rubio. Cuban raft baby with half a brother—lost—and half a life—lost—and half a Void keeping her half in the world. I'm sorry. You tried to help me and I did this to you.

...

I thought this would... I thought it would be an act of charity. The knife, the rope. This was supposed to free her, unburden her. She tried so hard to help me and I... I just hurt her again. Selfish to the end and beyond...

...

I wish I could undo this. I wish I could go back and knock my ass out for being so stupid, such a dumb, fucking self-pitying loser. I wish I could go back and never meet you. I wish I could go back and... be better? Let myself be helped? I don't know. How is it that I know I've fucked up, so, so badly, but I don't know how to fix it? I wish... I just wish...

...

Can I grant wishes? Can I magic this better?

...

I'm so sorry. None of this had to happen. I'm so sorry.

...

I did this.

...

I brought us here.

...

Just...

...

Regret.

...

...

...

I guess blaming myself is merely further self-indulgence. I couldn't be a saint and now I cope by giving myself too much credit as a villain? No. Of course not... I was just a drag. That's it. And, even now, I center on myself, when she's already...

...

If I... stop being. If I go back, what happens to her?

...

What happens to Emma if I go back?

...

Would I hold her up?

...

...

...

Paul? Are you there, Paulie Baby? Is this where you went?

...

Have you heard the one, Paul, about the boy and nothing?

...

All this time, I thought it was you. I thought you were with me, listening. I told you every joke I know, none of them funny, thinking it would... I don't know. Keep you around? Remind you that I'm still here, thinking of you and waiting? Maybe even bring you back. Don't you remember all those terrible jokes? All this...

...

And there's nothing there.

...

...

Good one.

Fuck off.

...

...

...

Can I undo this?

. . .

Can I go back, but earlier? Before? Can I change what happened?

It is not in my nature.

But I can see everything?

. . .

. . .

. . .

What happens to her if I go back?

. . .

Emma. Emmadora. I'm sorry.

And there's Jace, playing with the fastest, smallest, reddest car on a hospital floor. He tells Paul the dumbest, reddest jokes he can think of to keep him from noticing Mom's ragged breath, trying to keep himself from noticing.

. . .

And there's Emma, trespassing outside a midnight coffee shop that closed six hours ago. She has a foot out the door already and doesn't try to hold on but, still, she's holding, or held, and the night wraps around her with a wintery love I hope she feels.

. . .

And there's Jace, surrounded by people he's learned to hate, pushing the button to incinerate all that's left of his baby brother, still pretending he never heard Mom weakly call for her Jace Baby and then nothing else ever again.

. . .

And there's Paul. And there's Dad. And there's Jorge. And there's Valentina, Tabitha, Eric, Wendy—I don't know any of them. And there are countless others, scattered throughout all of existence, strangers to me and each other, utterly unlike but for the uniform me inside them. And there's everything. Or nothing. There's the incessant unpresence of unending emptiness.

Void.

I'm still here.

...

Just as well. It's so tiring being me, right?

...

I make the effort to remember what it is to be tired. And I am it. I'm afraid I won't find it again if I forget. I'm afraid to go to sleep, afraid I wouldn't know how to get back. Even these fears must be constructed from the ground up out of abstractions.

...

Each day here—the here itself—is a fiction, woven from threads of memory and oblivion. It takes a titanic effort to construct days, and take things one of them at a time. It's harder still to experience it all, knowing I'm powerless to change it. It would be easier to not perceive anything.

Void.

I know.

...

I know...

...

There's everything, from beginning to end, end to something beyond. Every space in every moment begs for an equal share of my attention and, God, it's a painful effort to focus on a here and now that only seems to exist to me because I insist it does. I'm afraid to lose my place in time, to not be able to find now once it's gone. I'm afraid to lose what may be my only way back.

...

But I slip sometimes. Some pieces stand out when my focus is broken and everything descends on me all at once...

...

There's Danny, sacrificing a future to come home when no one would admit that he was needed. And another out of sheer bad luck. There's Angela and what the world owes her. There's Sebastian, mine all along, not getting very far at all in the end. And there's Jorge, missing on the corner, trying to pray under a breath at rock bottom, in part, in passing, for Jace.

...

There's the Dragon—real, after all, but just the one, all alone, dormant, trapped at the bottom of a deep, deep well. She dreams a furious dream of math and deep space, an escape velocity answer to the ultimate question. Even now, she cautiously sneaks up on a Jace that's left the building altogether, a Jace who didn't have the answers anyway. There's a joke in there somewhere.

...

There's Emma, a whole lifetime in my cold hand. And there's a life she manages to get through, more or less. There's Mom, young and healthy and brave and in love. There's what he did to you, and how it mixes you all up inside. There's Jace going back, when the hand empties, right back into that field, and Jace going on without her or you and trying to live a better life and doing just a passable job of it. And there's Jace eventually dying and not coming back to me.

...

And there's Emma. Today, she tells a boy she doesn't know very well that he doesn't get the girl, and how they both would laugh themselves to tears if they could see how right she is.

. . .

Every observation, every conjured thought, a painful mimic of a life Jace used to have, is punctuated by the bitter knowledge that he could have been there, actually been there. And he chose to not be.

. . .

And there's Emma. Today, she wants to stay in bed until tomorrow, but a growing kitten demands that she get up and keep moving and put food in the damn bowl. It's a life—not the one he took from her, but the most I can give.

. . .

I am Jace. I have to remember that. I have to remember.

. . .

And there's Emma. Today, she visits the lack of her whole family, carries them with her for the rest of the day and well into her dreams. I hold her. I wish I could do more. I tell her I hear her. She pretends not to hear.

. . .

I wish you could have met her.

. . .

And there's Emma. Today, while staring blindly into a frozen display case at the grocery store, she makes a new friend, one who isn't mine. I hold her. I whisper to her that it's okay to stay, okay to be happy. I can't blame her for not believing *me*, but I whisper all the same.

. . .

I hope you're out there somewhere, Paulie Baby. Somewhere beyond even my dark omniscience. I hope you can hear me. It's Jace. It's me. Do you remember? Your big brother, with the soldier eyes. You've heard this one before, right? I *really* hope you're out there, Paul. Because, if you're not, and there's nothing there, then who the fuck am I talking to?

...

And there's Emma. Today, she puts a child to bed and sneaks away to sit for just a little while in the shadows outside a coffee shop that's mine and closed forever. I hold her in my cold arms.

...

ACKNOWLEDGEMENTS

There are people who helped me, or at least believed in me at my most delusional. In particular: Ed, Austin, Maria, Karen, JD, Torrell, Swati. Others too.

There are creatives who inspired me, for better or worse. In particular: Ceschi, Qwel & Maker, Ray Bradbury, Terry Pratchett, Ye. Others too.

Thanks.

ABOUT THE AUTHOR

Ankur Bhanderi is just some guy. He lives, and he intends to make that everyone else's problem.

Internets:
www.ankurisgreat.com
@ankurisgreater

www.ingramcontent.com/pod-product-compliance
Lightning Source LLC
Chambersburg PA
CBHW050730180626
46814CB00002B/694